A BEAUTIFUL KNIGHT

 THE CURSED KINGDOM

HILDIE McQUEEN

USA TODAY BESTSELLING AUTHOR

OLIVERHEBERBOOKS

Cover art by Dar Albert, Wicked Smart Designs

Published by Oliver-Heber Books

0 9 8 7 6 5 4 3 2 1

Chapter One

DUNIMARLE CASTLE
CULROSS, SCOTLAND

Gavin Campbell clenched his jaw, steeling himself for the agony he knew was coming. Every time he ripped through the veil between the alter-world and modern-day Scotland, searing pain tore through him. Returning was even worse, a brutal wrenching that left him gasping, the force growing stronger with each leap, stripping him of any semblance of control.

But there was no turning back. If he ever wanted to escape the centuries-long torment that had shackled him, he had to endure it. The faintest glimmer of hope flickered on the horizon—a way out, a chance to break free—but it came with a heavy price. Doubt gnawed at him, whispering that this could be his last shot, and it would be anything but easy. Yet he had no choice. The clock was ticking, and his time was running out.

As he fell through a tunnel of twirling lights, a sensation like that of a wind both pushing and pulling came over him and Gavin squeezed his eyes shut. Keeping them open would not only make him dizzy, but very possibly throw up.

For decades, he and four others had been trapped in a twisted alter-world by the dark wizard Meliot, each day a fresh torment in a realm far from the reality they'd once known. Here, they were subjected to relentless torture, forced into fruitless quests, and haunted by Meliot's hollow promises of freedom—a freedom that seemed forever just out of reach. Desperation gnawed at him, his resolve worn thin, yet he knew he had to escape...or be lost to this nightmare forever.

This was the opportunity he and the other three men trapped had to grasp. Each of them had a different curse looming over them, a different obstacle and would require a different enchantress to break them free.

Though the woman who called to him was deeply entwined with his fate—likely the key to breaking his curse— Gavin couldn't bring himself to focus on his own freedom. As much as he longed for release, he was determined to first help the other three men who were also trapped.

To break his curse meant facing an impenetrable barrier of memories, a past he had spent lifetimes trying to forget, filled with shadows he dared not confront. The thought of it unnerved him more than the curse itself.

Preparing for what undoubtedly would be a very awkward landing as he'd never mastered the art of balance, Gavin grunted as he once again became corporeal and on cue stumbled and landed on something soft. Whatever it was began to flail.

"Aaah!" A muffled squawk came from under him.

Her muffled words didn't need to be heard clearly to know they were curses as the person struggled. Unfortunately, his body was like an unmovable stone as Gavin became accustomed to being in a different place. Not only that, but it felt as if his muscles and tendons pulled away from his bones, the pain just a hair below intolerable.

Grunting and groaning, Gavin tried his best to roll off of the woman he'd landed on, recognizable by the few strands of fiery red hair sticking out from under him.

As fate would have it, he'd fallen atop of Sabrina Lockhart—of all people—who was meant to be his rescuer, assuming he didn't end up killing her first. The fiery woman was destined to break the spell that bound him and three others, trapping them for eternity in the alter-world.

The pain subsided as quickly as it came, and he finally managed to roll and sit on the floor, still unsure of his ability to stand.

After a brief struggle, Sabrina scrambled to her feet, her eyes flashing with annoyance as she motioned around her wildly. "Look around you, Goldie, this room is huge. Did you have to land on me? You could have killed me, you oaf!"

Too stunned to move, Gavin watched her from his sitting position on the floor.

The beauty glared down at him, arms crossed, foot tapping, eyes narrowed. "I don't get this whole willing yourself places, but it would seem you should be able to pick the place to land."

Coming to his rescue, Laird Tristan McRainey, who had also been trapped with him in the alter-world until recently, held out a hand. Gavin grabbed it and got to his feet.

"Are you all right Gavin?" Gwen, Tristan's partner, asked, pushing past a still glowering Sabrina.

Gwen gave her sister a patient look. "He didn't do it on purpose. It's not like they can specify where they materialize. You should be kinder. As you can see, the poor man is in pain."

"I am glad not to have hurt you. What Gwyneth states is true. I cannot choose exactly where to appear," Gavin added.

She merely grunted and regarded him for a moment. "It took you long enough. We've been trying to summon you for almost two weeks."

"That is strange, I did not sense anything," he replied honestly, locking eyes with her. For a moment, something flickered in her gaze, almost as if she wanted to say something, but then she looked away.

"Please sit Gavin," Tristan motioned to a chair, while he went to pour drinks.

The Laird looked very different from the last time Gavin had seen him, now dressed in the style of the current time in denim pants and a long sleeve pullover. His hair was different as well, trimmed into a modern haircut.

Since they'd been trapped and forever locked in the sixteen hundreds, he and the others had barely changed their form of dress.

"How have you and the others been faring?" Tristan asked.

"It has been quiet as of late. They send their regards."

His friend regarded him warmly. "I'm glad to hear it. I thought perhaps you were off on one of Meliot's ridiculous challenges."

Since the beginning of their imprisonment in the alterworld, a malevolent and powerful wizard by the name of Meliot was forever dragging them into senseless quests, promising to free them if they conquered or survived. Of course, there were always schemes and last-minute changes that kept them from ever winning.

Still, they fought, using their skills as swordsmen, and gifts magically granted to some of them by a Scottish enchantress just before being trapped.

"Nay, he has not bothered us since you left." Gavin replied watching Sabrina who pulled her hair back, securing it away from her face. A tendril escaped, falling alongside her cheek distracting him from Tristan.

"I hope he hasn't found a way to keep you and the others from sensing the pull to come here and try to save yourselves," Tristan said, fixing his attention back on the matter at hand.

Gavin's gut clenched at the sense that soon Meliot would be up to something horrible. "I would not be surprised. It is strange that he has been so quiet since you left."

"Excuse me boys. Time is limited," Sabrina interjected getting their attention and facing Gavin. "Gwen and I have been working on spells and searching for other people who have claimed to have faced a dilemma like this. Seems it is not as rare as I expected. Of course most are written off as made-up tales, but there are a few that seem eerily similar to this situation."

Gwen nodded in agreement. "Our youngest sister Tabitha is not as well-versed as we are, but we will speak to her and ask that she come to assist as well."

"I expect we need to find enchantresses," Tristan clarified, "since we can only be helped by the person we're meant to be with. Our enchantments all involve matters of the heart."

Gwen nodded. "At the same time, it wouldn't hurt to get others who could possibly help."

"Well, it's obvious Goldie here," Sabrina motioned to Gavin with her head, "and I are not *meant to be*." She held up two fingers on each hand, making air quotes.

"If he felt the pull, and you are the only other enchantress here, then it must be you who summoned him." Tristan insisted.

Sabrina rolled her eyes and let out an indignant huff. "I am not an enchantress."

"No one else is here?" Gavin asked looking around the room, enjoying Sabrina's fiery nature.

"No one with the gift of magic," Gwen replied. "Edith, has moved into town." She referred to Tristan's elderly descendant who had claimed Tristan as her son when he escaped the enchantment so that he could reclaim his properties and money wisely invested by the women in his family.

"There is Fiona," Tristan told them.

Both women huffed at the same time. "Good luck with that one," Sabrina said, crossing her arms.

"Who is this Fiona?" Gavin asked, noticing Gwen press her lips together, an arched eyebrow directed at Tristan.

"Er, she's a distant relative," Tristan told him. "She is

visiting. I am sure she has no gift of magic," his friend quickly added.

"We've wasted enough time." Gwen took Tristan by the hand, leading him out of the room while giving Sabrina a pointed look. "Get as much information as you can. The more you can get from Gavin, the easier it will be to come up with a spell to free him."

Looking around, Gavin noted that he and Sabrina were now alone.

"Might as well get started," Sabrina told him, rounding a desk and sitting. An obvious ploy to put distance between them. Gavin almost laughed.

He was well aware most women found him unsettling. The fact that he was a person of incomparable beauty was a fact, not conceit. His looks had always been more of a curse than a blessing throughout his life. To be admired for being attractive did not mean it brought respect. Quite the opposite. People expected him to be arrogant, of diminished intelligence and untrustworthy.

Although unsettled at his sudden appearance, Sabrina had never openly admired him. According to Tristan, she took portraits of beautiful men and women as a profession. He didn't quite understand the intricacies of how it worked, but his friend informed him she was wealthy from it.

Perhaps it was being surrounded by beauty that made it easier for her to act normal around him. Gavin liked it, it felt refreshing.

She glanced at him and then looked down at a contraption that had several lines of small squares. Her fingers tapped over the squares quickly as she studied a lighted frame.

He watched her work, the long red strands seemed to have a life of their own, more loosening from the clip and spilling forward, framing her heart shaped face.

Curious, Gavin stood and moved closer to see what she did. "What is this?" He pointed at the item her hands rested on.

"That's close enough Goldie, don't come nearer. I know all about those seduction powers of yours and I'm not taking any chances."

He ignored her warning and moved just a bit closer to look at the top part of the contraption. "What are you doing on that?"

"This is called a laptop computer. When I press down on the keys, the letter appears on the screen. It's like writing, but faster," she said pointing at the item in front of her.

After watching letters appear on the lighted frame, he lowered to a chair. It was a new experience for him, a woman who didn't try to immediately seduce him. A welcome reprieve of sorts, although it was strange that the woman who would hopefully save him could possibly be immune.

The fact she seemed not to be affected by his looks could be an obstacle to breaking his curse, which was something he'd have to contend with later.

Sabrina was not an approachable sort. Instead, he would describe her as prickly and ill tempered. Not quite unfriendly, but although much shorter than him, she managed to seem to look down her pert nose at him

"So," Sabrina began, looking up at him. "Let's begin trying to figure out the key to breaking you out."

"What is your full name Goldie?"

"Gavin Kendrick Campbell, Laird of Clan Campbell of Lochlann."

"Laird?" Her eyes lifted to look at him. "Impressive. Were you married? Any children?"

"Nay." he stood, feeling uneasy at discussing his family.

"Siblings?"

"Yes, two brothers. I also had a sister. All younger."

"I assume one of your brothers became the new Laird."

"Not for many years. My brother John eventually did. My uncle John Campbell took over as laird after I disappeared."

"I've heard of him. Well, there were several John Campbell's, weren't there? Every Laird Campbell becomes a Duke of Argyle right? Were you a duke?

"Nay, the title belonged to my uncle and cousins. And to answer your question, yes there were several laird's named John Campbell."

"Your clan was, er, is, one of the largest, most powerful clans in Scotland."

Immediately anger surfaced and Gavin tapped it down mentally. When his uncle had taken over as laird, his mistreatment of the clan's people had caused a huge rift in the clan. When his younger brother came of age, he'd become laird of people who'd defected. Unfortunately, for decades there was feuding, even warring between the two factions. It had been almost a century before peace had finally returned to Clan Campbell. However, even to present day, the split remained.

The vile wizard Meliot had not only damned him to years of entrapment but had caused many deaths in his family.

A strong pull to return to the alter-world tugged and Gavin grimaced just thinking of what was to come.

"Unfortunately, I have to go."

"Already?" she came from around the desk, nearing him. "We've barely started. I promised Tristan to do my best to help you. I need more information."

"He will understand lass," he told her, holding her gaze. Moving closer slowly, so as not to alarm her, he stopped in front of her, forcing her to look up to him. Had he noticed how luscious her lips were?

Noticing his gaze, she gasped, her lips parting, but she did not move away. "Are you doing it?" she asked him breathlessly.

"Nay," he replied but moved closer. "I will not use my seduction powers on ye."

"Promise?" The breathless question caused his heartbeat to quicken.

"Aye."

The pull back to the alter-world became too strong to ignore. He grimaced. "I'll return as soon as I can, lass. I am nae sure why, but I am pulled strongly to return," he told her before leaping.

. . .

IN THE ALTER-WORLD, Gavin landed on his butt in a bush with a loud grunt.

"You suck at this," Padriag, the youngest of the trapped men, slapped his leg and bent over laughing. "I never get tired of watching you land after a leap."

Padriag, spoke modern English due to the fact that his ancestral home, in current day Scotland, had been converted into apartments and the younger tenants exposed him to it.

The knight continued laughing as he tugged on Gavin's arm. "Sorry, I know you're hurting, but going through the pain in a prickly bush can't help."

When Gavin was finally able to flop onto the solid ground, he kept his eyes closed, waiting for the throbbing to pass. Tears squeezed through his eyelids, gliding down his face while he clenched his jaw, until he could finally breath normally.

Niall MacTavish, another of the trapped men, stood by in silence. The Scotsman kept vigil, his gaze scanning the surroundings.

There was no time to waste, Gavin got to his feet, and they quickly headed to their keep. Never knowing what could be thrown at them by Meliot, they didn't dare linger away from the keep for longer than necessary. Unfortunately, for some reason, they had to go away from their fortress in order to leap.

The two men didn't ask any questions as they jogged down a path that cut through a dense forest. The forest in the alter-world was nothing like the world where they came from. Tree trunks were the color of pumpkins, the leaves a strange combination of greys and greens and grass a strange reddish color. To him, it seemed to be eternally autumn.

Although he knew once they got to their home the men would be anxious to hear news, he wouldn't have much to tell. The visit had been cut short.

"I was there but a few moments," Gavin called out.

Padriag gave him a worried look. "Something is wrong. The entire time you were gone, strange flashes of light appeared across the sky."

Meliot knew. Somehow, he could feel it—their escape from the alter-world hadn't gone unnoticed. The wizard was already stirring, preparing to unleash his fury upon them.

He glanced at Niall and Padraig. The fear in their eyes told him they knew it too.

And then the air around them began to shift.

CHAPTER TWO

S abrina frowned at the website on the laptop screen, her mind awhirl. It was extremely difficult to remain immune to Gavin, whether he promised he wouldn't use his power of seduction on her or not,

According to Tristan, Gavin had been enraged that, while the others were given strength, magic, healing and foresight, he'd gotten an utterly useless power.

Perhaps it had been useless in the alter-world, but here in the real one, he could definitely benefit from it. Although with his looks, he didn't need magic to seduce women.

In fact, it could prove detrimental to their quest for his freedom if she went all gaga over him and was unable to think straight. It was best that she take precautions from now on and ward herself against it.

He'd said he wouldn't use his powers on her, but desperate measures called for the breaking of promises. Understandably after decades he might resort to all manner of things to be free.

Despite the urgency of the situation, Gavin didn't give her the impression he was desperate to be rescued. Whether tapping into instinct, having a premonition, or whatever, Sabrina was positive there was something he was not revealing, perhaps a reason that made him reluctant to reveal how to break his curse.

Perhaps it was just the instinct to protect himself from disappointment. It was understandable after so long that the men would expect something bad to happen that would rob them of the opportunity of leaving, so they guarded themselves. Sabrina's chest constricted at considering the unimaginable horrors they'd been through, not just physically, but mentally as well.

She adjusted herself on the plush chair and continued the internet searches on Clan Campbell. Since beginning her work at the McRainey estate, she'd found the library to be the most comfortable place to work. She spent hours there reading and researching similar cases, including Tristan's. For the most part, she'd only received a scant few replies to inquiries into people involved.

It was a frustrating and slow process, but she was doggedly determined to see the project to the end. If nothing else, it was proving to be the strangest and most unforgettable experience of her life.

His was the largest clan, which seemed to have split several times into smaller groups. Finding a specific Campbell lineage in Scotland was akin to finding one for a Smith in the US. She needed more information; names of his siblings would have helped.

As part of the research, she'd visited Castle Campbell

once already, losing herself in the rich history of Clan Campbell. Her excitement had turned into being overwhelmed by so much information about the Campbells, the many divisions of the clan and conflicting historical data.

She'd left the trip with a headache and armfuls of books and maps.

When Gavin returned, she would be more dogged in her questioning of him. Her gut told her that whatever the obstacle was, it was something very personal to Gavin. If he was keeping something back, it wasn't fair to her or the others.

ANOTHER STUMBLING BLOCK was the spell she was working on. Upon coming to Scotland to help Gwen with Tristan, words had come to her immediately. At first, she'd thought it had to do with Tristan and Gwen, but their spell was totally different.

Closing her eyes, she slowed her breathing and concentrated on keeping her mind blank to allow for the right words to formulate. Once again, the same spell formed, and she spoke the words out loud while thinking of Gavin.

It was almost ridiculous to conjure him without a mental image, no description could ever compete with the man in person. Even thinking it sounded ridiculous, but he was the most beautiful person she'd ever seen.

As a fashion photographer, Sabrina had worked with some of the most attractive humans in the world. None could compare to Gavin Campbell.

Before meeting him, Tristan had told them of how he'd

caused all types of incidents wherever he went. Wives leaving their husbands, just for the opportunity to be with him, even if just one time; troubadours singing of the 'Fair Campbell', and the fact that during his time, being called Gavin-like was an expression of the highest compliment to a woman's beauty.

Ever skeptical and thinking it an exaggeration, she was struck speechless upon seeing Gavin for the first time. They were not exaggerations.

He seemed flawless.

Even with her trained eyes, accustomed to seeing the world's most beautiful people, she was struck speechless.

The Highlander was tall, golden and drop dead gorgeous. Every single thing about him was impeccable. Luscious golden hair accentuated long-lashed amber eyes, lush lips and sculptured jawline. Then there was his build, about six-three, broad shoulders, broad chest, muscular legs and taut ass. His voice was rich like chocolate and, of course, when he grimaced or smiled, deep dimples formed.

He did have one flaw. The man was a klutz. Sabrina smiled, shaking her head, recalling him not only landing on her, but tripping over things when he'd appeared before.

A perfect example of God's sense of humor at play.

"What the hell was all that ruckus?" Fiona, Tristan's cousin, stood at the doorway, her long brown hair pulled back into a ponytail, a yoga mat rolled under her arm. "I had to start my entire yoga routine over. My peace was demolished."

Sabrina stopped her involuntary eyeroll. "I tripped over my footstool earlier," she lied.

"For a simple stumble, sure was a lot of noise," Fiona insisted, ensuring Sabrina understood how disruptive she'd been. The twenty-year-old walked into the library, looking up at the bookshelves.

"I've never been in this room. All those books are probably crawling with dust and mold spores." She wrinkled her nose and shuddered, scurrying back towards the door. "My allergies cannot handle it. Well, I'm off to change into riding clothes and then head to the stables."

"As if I care," Sabrina mumbled after Tristan's cousin walked out. Edith McRainey had apologized profusely to Tristan and Gwen when informing them of Fiona's upcoming visit, describing her as a bit spoiled.

An understatement of epic proportions.

Fiona had arrived two days later, expecting her luggage to be unpacked, her clothing pressed and put away and ordering about the two new staff members, hired specifically for her visit, huffing if they moved slower than she expected.

After brief introductions to Tristan, Gwen and Sabrina, she announced her desire to head to the stables immediately where she'd meet her trainer. Apparently, she was a competitive rider of sorts, who'd convinced Edith to allow her to not only house her two horses at the estate stables, but to also to allow her and her trainer to live on the estate while she trained for two weeks, prior to her competition.

At the time, Tristan was still trapped in the enchantment and Edith had not hired Gwen yet, so the woman saw no reason to decline her niece's request.

A ding alerted her to new email. Several more emails came in quick succession, all regarding upcoming photo shoots. After postponing shoots for two weeks, she was almost at the limit of how long she could stay away from her booming business.

She cringed just thinking of how long it would take her to catch up.

The only saving grace was Tammie, her youngest sister, whom she'd hired and was proving to be an amazing assistant.

Unfortunately, Tammie could not take the photos. She'd tried to recommend other photographers, but most of Sabrina's clients demanded that she be the one behind the camera.

An errant curl fell across her brow, and she brushed it away, her gaze shifting back to the computer.

"I have to get you out from under Meliot's spell Gavin Campbell, because my work cannot wait forever." As she spoke, a thought came to mind.

If Gavin was the man she was meant to be with, could she ever give up all she worked so hard for in order to be with him?

She didn't think so.

CHAPTER THREE

With little to do, the men often gathered in the main living space of the keep. It was split in two. A portion had several couches, comfortable chairs and a fireplace. There was a large table they dined at on the same side. In the other half, Padriag had conjured a pool table and had taught them all to play. He'd also created a contraption the young man called a "basketball hoop." Only Padriag used that.

At that moment, the men listened with interest as Gavin told them about his brief visit.

"So you're saying, Sabrina, the enchantress, is not affected by your looks?" Padriag gaped at him, eyebrows raised. "Well, there's a first. I can't believe it. Mental!" He made strange gestures on both sides of his head as if mimicking explosions.

Used to the young knight's use of modern English, Gavin nodded. "Aye, if anything, I swear the lass utterly dislikes me." He leaned back in the chair and crossed his arms.

"That is really a problem for you," Liam sneered at him. The English knight shook his head looking around the room at the other men. "Why are we wasting time on this drivel? You have the power of seduction, Gavin. Obviously next time you return, that is what you will do. The sooner she falls in love with you, the sooner your enchantment ends and the sooner we're rid of you."

Everything about the Englishman grated. Gavin leaned forward while replying through clenched teeth. "The sooner I stop seeing your pale face on a daily basis, the better my life will be as well."

"Guys?" Padriag waved his hands until they turned towards him. "Gavin, how does Tristan fare?"

"He fares well," Gavin replied recalling the way Tristan and Gwyneth exchanged loving looks. "Verra well actually. I truly believe he is in love. But he is not as happy as we would think. He's not stopping long enough to be at peace. Instead, he's working diligently to free us. I could tell by his demeanor, he carries a heavy burden of guilt, at being the first one free."

"Any progress that ye can tell?" Niall asked, his gaze moving to each of them. "I wish each of ye can be freed soon."

Gavin started to remark that he, too, should be freed, but he decided against it. Niall had no wish to be freed. He'd lost his family, a wife and children upon being trapped. Of them all, he'd lost the most.

"There is a third sister." That got all their attention, the men began speaking at once until Niall held his hand up signaling they should return their attention to Gavin.

"Tabitha, the youngest sister, is in America. Sabrina alluded to summoning her to Scotland. Although I was gone hours from here, I was only there a matter of minutes, and was not able to find out when she will arrive."

"Why did I not know about this?" Liam asked.

Padriag frowned. "I believe Tristan mentioned it once in passing. She's not an enchantress if I remember correctly."

"Whether she is or not, in Sabrina's opinion, she could be part of the key to breaking our enchantment," Gavin clarified.

"Three sisters," Padriag whispered. "We should find out if they have female cousins. Who's to say there isn't a lass for each of us?" At his comment the men chuckled.

"I believe Tabitha will be my enchantress," Padriag announced.

"Is that so," Gavin asked him, the young knight making him smile. "What if she's the ugly sister? There can't possibly be three fair sisters."

Not dissuaded, Padriag stood up and bowed to a chair. "My dear enchantress, Tabitha Lockhart, I am Sir Padriag Clarre, your knight in shining armor."

Gavin shook his head at the young man's antics. Even Niall broke into a rare smile. Liam, however, glowered at them, before getting up and walking towards the doorway.

"Perhaps the enchantress is for you," Gavin said to the Englishman. "Some women prefer a man who writes poetry and plucks flowers." Liam's body tensed.

"Nah, once she learns my sword is broader, I will be the next to be saved by a willing woman," Padriag said, a broad smile split his face as he joined Gavin in poking fun at Liam.

"Perhaps broader, but not as long." Liam replied, still not turning, his irritation evident. The Englishman never seemed to take jests well. Gavin considered it the curse of being English.

"Ah, but you see," Padriag continued, "the sisters prefer real men. Scottish men. If I need to keep an eye out for any competition, my attention is on Niall."

At the comment Niall huffed noncommittally.

"I believe you're right Padriag," Gavin told him. "The lasses do prefer true men."

When Liam tackled him, Gavin was not caught by surprise. The Englishman had a terrible giveaway. He always stomped his foot, prior to attacking. Gavin was able to roll on contact, hooking his arm around Liam, sending the Brit flying across the room.

When Liam landed, he immediately jumped up, this time with a different target in mind. Unlike Gavin, Padriag was caught unaware, busy laughing at Liam's first attack. They rolled across the floor, a tangle of arms and legs. After a couple of punches were thrown by each of them, Gavin and Niall stepped in and pulled them apart.

Niall grabbed Padriag up in a bear hug as the young red-faced knight yelled obscenities at Liam.

"What the fuck is wrong with you Brit? You need someone to kick your ass good. You need to learn to take a joke," Padriag yelled, then gave up struggling.

Liam twisted out of Gavin's grasp, turning to him, obviously still quite angry. "Who says I'm not the one that should be visiting the fair Sabrina? Maybe it's time I go. I have much to tell her about her 'knight.' Tell me Campbell, how do you plan to engage in lovemaking when ye can't bear to be touched sexually?"

He barely got the last word out when Gavin's fist connected with his gut and Liam bent over letting out a loud grunt.

"That is enough." Niall turned at Gavin. "I don't know why you and Liam hate each other so. The Brit allows his temper to get the best of him, and you let his words get to you."

Both Liam and Gavin glared at each other, breaking eye contact to look at Niall, who seemed to deflate. "We may never leave here. Here we have little control over anything. No matter what we do, little good it does."

The Scot's black hair reflected the flames as Niall stooped to stoke the wood in the fireplace. Over the years, they'd grown to understand each other as much as they knew themselves, whether it was Niall's continuous grief or Padriag's lighthearted way of dealing with the entrapment. Then there was Liam, who used anger as a shield to keep his true emotions at bay. As for himself, Gavin blocked all thoughts of his past by concentrating on filling each day with whatever activity he could. Despite hating Meliot and the useless quests he sent them on, it was a respite from the taxing task of blocking out memories of the past.

Gavin went to stand next to Niall. "If I am to be next in the sequence of leaving, then I am not sure how it will happen. It means Sabrina must fall in love with me. Then there is the other part. The power of seduction is only physical."

"Love is not all physical Gavin, but it is a big part of it.

Wait and see, until the time comes. I am sure it will become clear," Niall replied and met his gaze. "Whatever the other portion is, together you will find a way."

He suppressed a shudder and blew out a breath. "Padriag should be next to leave, not me. I do not think to be able…"

Being touched was tolerable, but the mere thought of a woman's seducing touch shattered him, dragging him back to a dark past where survival meant using violence as his only defense.

Niall kept his attention at the fire. "I understand that there are reasons why the curse was placed on you, but with the right spells and wards, many things can be overcome."

Gavin lowered his head.

The curse seemed simple to overcome.

The deepest love your lover has ever known.
An intimate touch that reaches the soul.
Surrendering total and complete freedom over your body,
offering yourself freely, without hesitation or compulsion.
Find your truth in the transformation.

For years before the enchantment, he'd been celibate. The thought of a lover's touch was unfathomable.

A fate he'd accepted, but now, it could stand in the way of the other men's freedom.

CHAPTER FOUR

"This is crazy, I can't do it. I have a job to return to, people depending on me to make a living." Sabrina sat forward on the edge of her bed, pleading her case to her sister.

"I can't just sit around waiting for Goldie to decide to appear. I'm sorry; I really need to fulfill my contracts and save my reputation." She flopped back onto the bed.

Unruffled, as usual, Gwen smiled at her patiently. "You have enough money, Sabrina. You told me yourself the current photo shoot was delayed. Give it at least another two weeks. You can afford to pay the crew for their time."

Sabrina nodded. What her sister said was true. Her photography was a labor of love, and she was damned good at it. That she was paid very well was an added bonus. Her main problem was that, unlike Gwen, she didn't give two shits about having any kind of magical gift.

Yes, it came in handy at times and it was nice to help

people, but at the same time, to her it was more of a hobby, not something she relied on.

At Gwen's pointed look, she let out a sigh. "Most of them can probably do other work while they wait. With the delay, I'm sure they have jobs lined up. Other than Tammie, who is working."

"You can't put a price on the freedom of these men, can you?" Gwen asked.

Chastised, Sabrina sat back deflated. "You're right. I know. It just seems impossible at times."

"Something else is bothering you, isn't it?" her insightful sister inquired.

Her first instinct to lie fell away when she looked at Gwen. "I am having a hard time reconciling one portion of this whole curse thing. That whoever breaks them free is who they are destined to be with. I am not ready for that."

"I totally get that," her sister began. "We don't know the specifics of Gavin's curse, and it doesn't necessarily mean a commitment or a lifetime."

Although true, the idea of destiny made her uncomfortable. Not that Sabrina was against a relationship, but she preferred it to be something more traditional. Like dating apps.

Gwen's lips curved and her eyes twinkled with mirth. "I doubt it would be hard to fall for him. Come on, he's a walking dream." Her sister bit her bottom lip, closed her eyes pretending to swoon. "Tristan is gorgeous, and I wouldn't trade him for the world, but I have eyes and Gavin is breathtaking. Isn't he?"

Sabrina nodded reluctantly. "Exactly and that's another point. Can you imagine falling in love with someone who looks like that? Women falling over backward, all kinds of propositions. I would be in jail every other week for yanking people's hair out by the roots."

Something in her chest tightened. "He'll probably not stick around for long anyway. So, I'm not sure why I'm stressing."

Her sister surveyed her for a long moment. "He's not Tyler. It's been over a year Sabrina. Give yourself a chance to fall in love again."

"I have. I've been on lots of dates!" Sabrina exclaimed.

"You date male bimbos, and not one amongst the men you've dated lately was your type." Her sister laughed. "Remember Zinc? He couldn't figure out why we kept asking him if he ever was cold. And who names their kid Zinc?"

Sabrina cringed at the memory. "Zinc is hot and was good in bed." She wagged her eyebrows at her sister, before admitting, "Out of bed, he was a bit of an airhead. It was annoying that he refused to wear anything other than his underwear unless totally necessary. Good on the eyes, but too naked. He named himself Zinc. It was his professional name."

Both giggled.

Gwen stood to leave. "When Gavin reappears, ask him the specifics of his enchantment, and if part of the way to help him is to fall in love, then you can freak out."

Once her sister was gone, Sabrina stood and went to the

window and peered out. The day was rainy, a constant drizzle since that morning. It had been months since she'd thought of her fiancé. Tyler had broken off their relationship just weeks before their wedding, claiming he wasn't ready. She'd begged him not to leave, had acted in ways that were embarrassing to think about now. Sobbing, clinging to him, asking for a second chance, claiming not able to imagine life without him.

To his credit, he'd been visibly upset, and tried to explain why he wanted to end things. She'd not allowed him to talk, her anger and heartbreak overridden by pride. In retrospect, he had been true to himself, not staying in a relationship because of guilt.

Sabrina didn't remember much about the weeks right after Tyler had moved out. She'd thrown herself into work and did not take a day off for months. Through it all, her sisters had been an unmoving circle of support when she'd needed it the most. Finally, when the haze of heartbreak began to fade and Sabrina emerged from it, she'd not felt stronger, as some people claimed, but glued back together. The cracks were still there, like weathered puzzle pieces.

And in her opinion, it wouldn't take much for her heart to be easily broken again.

"Are ye well?" Gavin's voice shook her out of her thoughts. He hovered near the doorway, a frown barely marring his perfect features. "Ye seem troubled."

"Ah you returned." She couldn't get used to this whole sudden appearance thing. Sabrina waved his words away, assuming her nonchalant demeanor.

After silently warding herself against unwelcome magic,

she motioned for him to follow to the bed. He went to a chair next to the bed and lowered himself onto it.

She sat on the edge of the bed and opened her laptop, barely glancing at him. This was not the time to get lured into admiration. Nonetheless, she could feel his intense stare.

"I have some direct questions for you. Since you tend to vanish quickly, let's start."

He nodded. "Very well."

"How is your enchantment to be broken?"

Gavin cleared his throat. He seemed uncomfortable. "First we must find the spell."

"I understand that part. What else?" She kept her voice even, almost as if he were one of her clients.

"Ye must make love to me."

"Just sleep with you?" She grinned. "Not fall in love with you?"

He slid his gaze to the bed. "That may not be necessary."

"Thank God!" This time she smiled broadly at him.

Confused, he frowned at her. "Ye seem happy? Why? Are you already in love with someone?"

Sabrina continued to smile. "Oh no, I'm not currently in love with anyone. I just don't want to fall in love with you." She noticed his look of confusion intensify. "Nothing personal Gavin—but would you like to fall in love with a beautiful man?"

"Nay, I don't want to fall in love with any man." He frowned.

"Okay, I phrased it wrong. I don't know how things were back in the sixteen hundreds, but nowadays, you are the epitome of the perfect man. Women will kill themselves to get at you. Whatever woman you choose as your partner will have to deal with you constantly being approached by other women. Probably men too."

"It doesna matter," he told her locking gazes with her. "I will never be unfaithful."

A chill ran through her and she crossed her arms. "Okay. Umm, back to the enchantment. First the spell, and then have sex...er, make love." She typed in the information into her notes, closed the laptop and pushed it aside.

"Come." She got up and moved toward the bed. "I think I got the spell, then we'll have sex and see what happens. I don't have a problem with casual sex. It will be fun."

Gavin got to his feet, looking as if he was prepared to run. With wide eyes he looked at the bed with what could only be described as terror.

"Is there something else?" Sabrina replied confused. "Take your clothes off and come to the bed." She told him speaking slowly.

"I didn't explain the terms of the bedding to ye," Gavin told her, frozen to the spot where he stood, his eyes locked to the bed. "You have to make love to *me*," he said emphasizing the word 'me.'

"So, I do all the work. Are you sure you're not making that part up?"

He nodded, lips pressed together.

Sabrina exclaimed, "Okay I think you're making that up."

"Why would I do that?" He asked, anger replacing wariness. "I do not lie."

"Fine, whatever," Sabrina was actually looking forward

to sex with him. He was hot and well built. "What's holding you back?"

"There is another part that I don't understand." Gavin seemed to relax now that she'd moved back to sit down on a chair. "The words say that we must find the truth in the transformation."

She'd have to be patient. "Tell me the curse. Word for word."

His Adam's apple bobbed, and he nodded. "The deepest love your lover has ever known. An intimate touch that reaches the soul. Surrendering total and complete freedom over your body, offering yourself freely, without hesitation or compulsion. And find your truth in the transformation."

"Wizards love riddles, don't they?" Sabrina huffed and pointed to the chair. "Pull that chair closer and sit. Repeat the curse so that I can type it in. I'll have to go over it with Gwen."

At his look of relief, she almost rolled her eyes. Surely having sex with her would not be that hard of a task. She met his eyes. "Before you go, I want to try the spell that I have written. I'm curious to see what happens, if we sense it's the right one."

She scooted to the edge of the bed and held out her hands palms up on her lap waiting for him to place his on top; he looked at her hands hesitantly before placing his large hands on hers.

When their hands touched, Sabrina inhaled sharply and prayed her ward held. Just his touch would have buckled her knees if she'd been standing.

"Turn it off Goldie." She gritted her teeth.

"I am not doing anything." He replied impatiently. "My name is Gavin."

She ignored him and closing her eyes, began to chant the spell she'd memorized.

By earth, by air, by fire, by sea,
I call upon the power to set thee free.
Chains unseen and binding tight,
Shatter now, by ancient light.
By flame that burns and water's flow,
The captive heart begins to grow.
No longer held by fear or might,
I summon freedom's endless flight.
By star and moon and sun above,
I break the bonds with strength and love.
The curse is dust, its hold is gone,
By will and word, the spell is done.

Gavin's grip tightened and she opened her eyes. He seemed to be in some sort of trance. His eyes half closed, long lashes fluttered, his mouth slightly parted, he let out a breath before opening his eyes. The amber eyes darkened just enough to make the golden flecks almost sparkle. She lost the ability to breathe. Her sister was correct, he was definitely breathtaking.

His eye met hers briefly before looking past.

Again, the look of pure fear that could not be mistaken for anything else returned.

Not mere jitters.

The man was scared to death.

"You felt something didn't you?" she asked, not understanding why he wasn't elated. "The room seemed to tilt and then swayed. Did you feel it?"

He frowned, looking at their hands still joined. "I do. I have to go."

When he didn't pull his hands away, Sabrina didn't move either. Then it struck her. It had probably been hundreds of years since he'd been with a woman. Perhaps he needed time to adjust to being touched. She slid her right hand out and ran her fingers along the top of his slowly, keeping an eye on him. His hand was large, a warrior's hand. Although his palm was rough, the skin on top of his hand felt soft. She traced a circle softly around each knuckle. He watched intently, not moving.

"Gavin," she said continuing the movement of her fingers on his left hand. "How about we take it slow? Start with touching. I'm here for as long as it takes."

His look of relief didn't surprise her. The man *was* scared! Her heart softened at the sight of his grateful smile. And she steeled herself against it.

"Thank you."

"What is happening with the others?" Sabrina asked, her fingers continuing to trace from his hand to his lower arm. "Have any of them felt anything yet?"

"Nay. I mentioned yer sister to them."

She couldn't stop the surge of protective instinct. "I am sure Tammie won't be one of their saviors. Tristan and Gwen are already searching for others with gifts to see if they can come and help."

"That is good. I will inform the men. Tell Tristan things

remain calm with us for now. There have been no quests or attacks."

"Tell me something. Be honest. How do you really feel? Are you ready to be freed?"

Gavin studied their hands. "There are days when I wish for nothing more than to be free of that world. I understand the sooner I am freed, the faster we can free the others." He'd not said how he actually felt, but she let it go.

Slowly he flexed the fingers of his right hand, circling hers. He took a sharp breath but didn't let go.

There was something he held back, a reason for the fear that had nothing to do with her or even sex. Whatever it was made the curse hard to break. She'd have to study the curse word for word.

"Gavin, this "making love" condition. There is something difficult about it for you, right?"

He slid his hands away from hers. "I can make love to a woman."

When he stood, she rose with him and placed her hand on his arm insuring she kept the touch neutral. He stared at her hand but didn't move away.

He grimaced. "The pull is getting strong."

Sabrina grabbed the laptop. "So, you do not fear love-making, but I suspect it is more the way the act is performed that breaks the curse?"

It was slight, but he nodded.

"Good. Now, I think we should also consider location. Can you get yourself to your ancestral home?"

"I have gone there in the past, so yes." He let out a soft

grunt and grimaced again, but didn't disappear to the alter-world.

Sabrina could tell he barely hung on. "Hurry back. I have an idea. Come to where I summon you."

"I will." Locking gazes with her, he nodded once and vanished.

CHAPTER FIVE

Gavin's landing was smoother, unfortunately the sounds of swords clashing didn't allow for any time of relief at landing in soft grass. Pushing past the searing pain, he rolled onto his back and opened his eyes. Bad timing, a Minotaur's ax lowered right at his throat.

Death had arrived. Gavin's eyes flew wide as time seemed to slow and a sword blocked the descent of certain death.

Niall flung himself at the creature, barely moving it. Centaurs, half horse, half man, were exceptionally strong, but the Scot somehow managed to keep it at bay.

Liam fought a few feet away, the Englishman's elegant movements fluid as he battled against another creature.

When Gavin's sword landed next to him with a thump, Liam grabbed for it. Padriag a few steps away, fought another centaur. Long bladed daggers in each hand, the young knight's arms moved so fast they blurred.

"Behind you," the knight yelled at Gavin without turning.

Jumping to his feet, Gavin swung his sword at the approaching Minotaur barely missing him when the creature leaped backward. Planting his feet, he held his sword with both hands preparing for the black creature's advance, out of the corner of his eye he saw a centaur approaching from his right.

Relying on instinct alone, Gavin began to battle. Between blocks and thrusts, he kept an eye on the others. He dispatched the centaur, a loud scream ripping out as the creature evaporated. The sounds of battle seemed to fade as he turned to face off against the Minotaur.

Gavin, an unusually tall man, was still a head shorter than the black muscular creature that advanced toward him, snorting in anticipation. Thankfully, when battling, any clumsiness vanished, and his extensive training took over.

Gavin began fighting the beast. They were evenly matched, and he found himself actually enjoying the fight. If it wasn't for the life-or-death portion, he wouldn't mind clashing with enemies more often.

Seeing an opening for a death strike, he swung with all his might. Just as he would have struck, the creature disappeared causing Gavin to nearly fall over.

"Oh yeah!" Padriag danced a jig, then began sliding backwards, wiggled his hips and pointed a dagger toward the sky. "I'm bad, I know it." He sang.

Gavin shook he head at the young knight's antics.

The celebration was short-lived.

"Liam's gone," Niall told them.

Padriag's celebration ended abruptly. "Shit."

"That's enough." Meliot called out just as the last snap of the whip tore into Liam's flesh.

Manacles that hung from the ceilings in the cold stone-walled room were locked around his wrists. No longer able to stand, Liam hung limply, his knees hovering just above the blood-stained floor.

A bucket-full of cold water drenched his face, someone pulling his head back by his hair and pouring more down his throat. He choked, coughing violently.

He could barely make out Meliot's shape, since the cavernous room was choked with smoke from an enormous fireplace.

The wizard came closer to him, giving him a pitying look. Tall and lean, the ancient sorcerer still looked to be middle-aged. He was an evil man who obviously relished being a spectator of torment by the glee on his face.

"You have no idea why you are here do you?" Meliot leaned into his ear. "I think I will let you try to figure it out on your own."

Liam head butted the wizard, barely tapping him, too weak to do much damage.

The sting of a hard slap barely registered. It was nothing compared to what he'd already endured.

"You hit like a woman," he told the wizard only to get punched in the jaw so hard he saw stars. "Thanks. My head needed an adjustment," he said, spitting blood out, satisfied to see most of it land on Meliot's shoes.

The man's outfit was a cliché. He wore long robes and

pointy shoes, his beard and hair long and silver. If not for his predicament, Liam would have made a comment about it. But he was at a loss for a proper insult.

"What is her name?" The wizard spat out.

"Mabel. Betty. Amanda, or maybe Susan. I can go on all day, except no one is clarifying what woman you want me to name."

"The woman who is to try to break you free," The wizard replied running a fingernail into one of his lash wounds. Liam could hold back a moan.

When he remained silent, Meliot motioned for one of his minions to come near. The demon-like creature held a branding iron, the end of it, bright red. "Now, tell me the name."

Meliot didn't know who was to be freed. For whatever reason he seemed to think it was him. Liam wanted to laugh. Even if there was someone who would try to save him, Liam would die before revealing it.

THE DARKNESS BEGAN TO FADE, and Liam heard a low moan. Fighting his way back to consciousness, he realized the moans were his own. His sides ached, broken ribs the cause, no doubt. The pain of the fresh burns began to intensify, and he gritted his teeth, recalling not only how the creature branded him, but how he'd used the iron to hit him across the ribs until he passed out from the pain. As soon as he was free, he'd kill the little bastard.

Meliot never killed the knights, although, he did torture them until they wished for death. He was too evil to kill them and end their torment, as it was Meliot's source of entertainment.

He didn't recall telling the wizard anything and hoped he'd passed out before saying anything that could be used against them.

Why was he here? The one on the verge of escaping was Gavin, not him. The Scot felt the pull to the other side, not him. In truth, Liam doubted he ever would.

Glancing around discreetly under his lashes, he noted a guard by the door snored, his head hanging to the side. The other creature, the one who'd tortured him, was at a table, slumped over. Seemed even evildoers required rest.

His wrists burned from the irons around them, and he pushed up on his feet to allow some respite. It helped enough that he let out as much of a breath as he could with broken ribs.

Meliot never pulled them out of the alter-world whenever he decided to use them for sport, so Liam assumed that he currently found himself somewhere under the wizard's castle. Hopefully the others were on their way. He didn't relish another round with Meliot getting off at his expense.

Despite the animosity between himself and Gavin, the man would join Niall and Padriag in fighting with all their powers to rescue him. They'd made an oath to each other and had never once deviated from it. No matter what, they would always defend and fight for one another.

The creature at the table stirred and Liam went slack, closing his eyes.

CHAPTER SIX

Apprehension hung over the trio, as they made their way to Meliot's castle.

Red streaks lined the purple sky of the alterworld, the two suns partially covered by cloudlike puffs of grey matter.

Gavin held up a fisted hand, a silent signal for them to stop while pulling his own horse to a standstill. The distant rumble, like that of thunder, sounded, and Gavin jumped down placing his palm on the ground.

The ground vibrated with the pounding of hooves. Whoever or whatever came was moving closer.

Niall whistled softly and guided his horse into the woods; Gavin mounted and followed, Padriag behind him. A few yards into the thick forest, they dismounted and ducked behind trees. Padriag cast a spell, and the horses disappeared. They remained visible to keep track of each other.

Gavin crouched behind a large fallen tree, waiting for whoever or whatever came. Niall stood behind another tree, his sword drawn, while Padriag totally disappeared, holding the horses' reins and keeping the invisible animals calm. The young knight's ability to become invisible made it easier for him to hide, a necessity since his bright reddish hair could be hard to camouflage.

Armored men riding two by two came into view along the road they'd been on. It was hard to tell if they were human or not as they all wore helmets.

"Meliot's minions." Niall whispered. "We should follow."

Padriag conjured helmets to match those Meliot's guards wore and they donned them, mounted and followed behind.

Soon the Icing would take place, an occurrence in the alter-world in the region surrounding Meliot's castle when sleet, rain and ice fell with force. Not only was it impossible to see when caught outdoors but also hard to survive if left exposed as the temperatures fell to a deep freeze.

As they rode, Gavin steeled himself against the cutting wind. Soon a thick snow began. None of Meliot's soulless warriors seemed affected by the freezing sleet and hailstones pelting them.

"I think my dick just froze off," Padriag hissed, his teeth chattering. "Even with our extra layer of clothing under this ugly ass armor, I can't stop shaking."

"Be quiet," Gavin whispered back. "You'll attract attention." Although it was doubtful, between the pounding of horse hooves and the roaring of the wind, it was best not to take chances.

Meliot's dark grey castle finally came into view, the turrets looming over the frozen trees, guards on watch atop each one. Gavin scanned the surrounding area noting only several pairs of black wolves.

Sentries.

Meliot had rather lax security, no guards at the gates. It was obvious he never worried about intruders, probably gave more consideration to ensuring against breakouts. Because who the hell would voluntarily come to that godforsaken place?

If Liam was being held there, he would be subjected to torture just for Meliot's entertainment. Time was of the essence, lest their friend suffer greatly. Gavin looked to Niall and Padriag's tense faces, understanding they were thinking the same thing.

Meliot's warriors seemed to have the same assurance that no one would dare enter the castle because they didn't pay Gavin, Niall and Padriag any heed as they passed through the open gates.

The trio followed the warriors into the castle courtyard; mimicking what they did. Gavin noticed with relief that the warriors did not remove their helmets, as they split up and headed to different areas, some to a building past the court-yard others to what he assumed were the stables. There was nothing else in Meliot's castle courtyard. No bonfire nor animals other than the pair of wolves.

Warmed air swirled around them, as Padriag waved a hand in the direction of their horses. "Horses will be comfortable and can only be seen by us," Padriag whispered, motioning with his head to where their mounts that stood side-to-side.

Silently, they hurried to a door and Niall opened it. As

they followed a long corridor, there was nothing visible, so they hurried forward until reaching an archway. They stood at the top of a stairwell that spiraled down below the castle.

Niall looked to Padriag. "How long can you keep us from being seen?"

"Long enough," Padriag said. "The invisibility spell should hold long enough for us to free Liam and get back out."

"I hope this works, Meliot is not stupid, and he's probably expecting us," Gavin said.

When his friends disappeared before his eyes, Gavin held his hand up and saw nothing. Niall's soft whistle told them to begin moving down the stairs. Gavin went slowly, not wanting to accidentally bump into one of the other two.

Light hit them when someone opened the doorway and climbed the stairs. Gavin flattened himself against the damp stone wall holding his breath. The guard walked past him, seeming not to sense him or the other two.

Once they reached the bottom of the stairwell, the stench of human waste mixed with other things he didn't want to identify led them to a dungeon.

Gavin moved toward the right wall, scanning the dungeon while fighting the urge to throw up from the horrible smells. He reached under the helmet and pulled his shirt up around his nose. It barely helped.

Several cells lined the wall, each holding an unfortunate victim. He peered into the enclosures hoping to find Liam. Then, upon hearing Niall's soft signal, he moved toward another room.

In the larger room, the air was just as stagnant, but unlike the last, this one had some light, and a cage tucked in a corner.

Several bloodied tables were lined up, with all sorts of tools of torture on the tops. In the middle of the room, Liam hung by his wrists, his knees almost reaching the ground, head flopped forward. Gavin's stomach lurched at the sight. He fought not to rush forward and free him. Instead, he dragged his eyes away from Liam's sad figure and waited for Niall's signal.

There were two others present. A guard just inside the door sat slumped in a chair and a creature resembling a mouse sat at a table, its head atop its folded arms.

Gavin slowly made his way to the guard by the door, drew his dagger and sliced the man's throat. Niall had done the same to the rat creature, because a dark pool grew larger and larger under its head.

Liam was no longer visible, the only clue to what happened was the sound of feet shuffling. It meant Padriag carried the unconscious knight outside.

Once outside, Padriag would leap with him back to the keep. At least that was the plan.

"Let us go, quickly," Niall whispered.

Gavin dashed back up the stairs, a niggling tingle at the back of his neck. This was too easy, why weren't the doors leading past the cells to the outside being guarded?

The answer came quicker than he would have liked. Just as he reached the top of the stairs, he was slammed against the wall so hard that he tumbled all the way back to the bottom.

No longer invisible, he shook his head trying to clear it.

Tearing the helmet from his head, his eyes went wide. Gavin screamed, but it was silent.

AT ONCE HE began to shake, every ounce of his being revolting at the realness of where he found himself.

The soft strains of Arabic music being played on a quanan, a stringed instrument, drifted through the room. Vibrant rugs cushioned the floor beneath every step. The air, fragrant with incense, accented the opulence of the surroundings.

On a sideboard, platters overflowed with a bounty of exotic fruits while crystal decanters held sweet nectars that seemed to shimmer in the light emanating from dozens of intricate lanterns.

The canopied bed upon which he rested was draped in the finest linens, with pillows as plump and inviting as clouds.

Meliot's laughter echoed, and Gavin shook so hard his teeth began to chatter. He was frozen, barely able to breath. This couldn't be happening. His worst nightmare came to life. He fought to keep a scream that formed as terror filled him.

"What is the matter with you?" Nadia's dark eyes peered down at him. His only friend. "Are you having a bad dream?" The pretty girl shook her head, placing the decanter of scented oil down.

Gavin could not reply. He sat up, looking around. It couldn't be. He was back, somewhere in the Middle East. Everything remained the same, just like when he'd left, almost four hundred years earlier.

His hand shook as he reached up to move his hair away

from his face, only to stop as he noticed the metal slave band on his wrist.

"Gamil? Are you unwell?" Nadia came a bit closer, knowing better than to touch him. Gavin flinched, and tried to move away, but was hindered. It was then he knew he was chained by the ankle to one of the massive bedposts.

"Leave me Nadia, I wish to be alone."

"They come for you Gamil, I brought you this," Nadia held out an apple to him. He slapped it away. "Yabtaeid!" Go away was one of the few phrases he'd learned to say in Arabic.

"I am sorry, Gamil. Ye need to be prepared. There is to be a celebration." There was pity in her eyes when she looked at him and then Nadia hurried out of the room.

Gamil. How he hated that name. He'd been called that since arriving. It meant "beautiful" in Arabic.

Distraught, Gavin began yanking at the chain at his ankle, only to realize how much smaller he was. No longer muscular and broad, his arms appeared slimmer, his legs much leaner. Not caring, he continued pulling at the chain, the skin on his ankle tearing, blood staining the satiny bedding.

At the sound of the door opening, he became frantic, tugging and tearing at the chain. Two huge eunuchs entered and neared the bed.

Tears streamed down his face as he tried in vain to get away. With ease, one of the massive males held him against his broad chest, arms pulled back while the other removed the ankle iron.

Two women entered with clean linens. Without glancing at him, they began changing the bedding. He was lowered to stand, and the eunuchs held him as he struggled with all his might, kicking, biting and punching to no avail, the men took each hit without even a slight flinch.

The women removed his pants and tunic, and the men dragged him into an empty heavily perfumed bathing room, dunking him into a hot bath.

In the steaming water, he coughed and gagged as the women scrubbed him thoroughly and dunked him under to rinse off the soap. Once the bathing was completed, they held him down on a wooden slab, while hot wax was applied to his underarms, legs and groin, all traces of hair removed.

Finally, they rinsed him. By this point Gavin was so exhausted from fighting that he hung limp between the men. His ankle was bandaged with a red cloth and gold ankle jewelry wrapped to distract from the swelling. Finally, a golden colored, silk jeweled scarf was wrapped around his waist.

Finally, a now-docile Gavin was taken into another familiar room, one of the rooms that adjoined the sheik's living space.

There were several women present there in the room, sitting among pillows that had been placed along the wall. The women's expressions were like masks of pleasure, but their eyes were flat. When he met one of their gazes, the woman glared back.

She spoke under her breath in Arabic to the one next to her and although he wasn't fluent, he knew she was angry not to be chosen to share the sheik's bed that night.

His gut clenched, her animosity could only mean one thing.

The muscular eunuchs had to practically drag him to where the sheik was seated. He began to thrash and fight again.

Not this, not again.

Held between the large men, Gavin glared defiantly at the large turbaned male, who lounged on a ruby red rug, supported by pillows, women feeding him. A thick moustache covered most of the sheik's lips as they curved up in a patient smile. The man shook his head and laughed when Gavin kicked one of his captors, as if amused by a spoiled child.

The sheik waved for them to put him down across from where he sat. Shoved into pillows across from the turbaned man, Gavin fell back only to be pushed up into a seated position. A platter of sweet meats and fruit was placed in front of him, a large goblet of wine next to it. He didn't eat, but remained stock still, hoping to regain his strength, before they tried to take him to the bed.

Suddenly strong hands grabbed his face from behind, and his arms were pulled back. He tried to keep his mouth shut, but his jaws were forced open, and one of the girls poured wine down his throat. By the strange taste Gavin knew it was drugged because almost immediately he began to see colors flashing, and the room swayed.

Morsel after morsel of food was placed in his mouth and the flavors exploded, everything tasted astonishing delicious. No longer able to form a coherent thought, he yearned for another drink and reached for the goblet. Someone picked it up and brought it back to his lips. He drank greedily from it, enjoying the savory explosion on his tongue.

"He is ready."

Gavin heard the sheik speak, and considered reacting, but couldn't remember why he should.

Lifted to his feet, a floating sensation overcame him as he was laid back onto ruby red satin sheets.

CHAPTER SEVEN

"Gavin? Can you hear me?" Niall's voice was insistent, barely penetrating through the fog in his head.

His entire body shook from the freezing temperatures and Gavin pried his eyes open to see his friend's face looming over him. Sleet fell, most of it blocked by Niall's cape as he used it to shelter them.

"The Icing is in full force now," Niall told him, tucking his large cape around them, careful to keep from touching him.

Although he'd share a portion of what happened in his past, only Naill knew the entire story. The others had learned that when he was trapped in visions of his past, it was best not to be near, else chance being blindly attacked.

"If you cannot leap to the keep, we'll have to try to wait this out.

"Where are the horses?" Gavin asked, somehow forming the words in spite of his chattering teeth.

"I do not know." Niall replied, with a sharp shiver.

"I can leap. Go, now." At least hoped he could. The likelihood of surviving outdoors was slim if they remained since the Icing could last for an entire night.

Closing his eyes, Gavin concentrated on their home until finally the sensation of being pulled through space took over.

Both men landed outside the keep moments later. Niall stood immediately. The man, either impervious to pain or too damn stubborn to care, helped Gavin stand, half-dragging him toward the keep.

Although it was almost dusk, the mild temperature where they lived was a vast improvement over where they'd just been. Still both Niall and Gavin were chilled to the bone and shivering uncontrollably.

How long had he lain outside in the ice? His legs refused to work, wobbling under him like a newborn calf's. Niall's strong arm around him was the only thing keeping him upright.

At the touch of another human, he began shaking uncontrollably, and he fought to keep from shoving his helper away.

Once they entered the keep, Padriag helped Niall carry him in.

"He was outside for quite a while before I found him," Niall's gruff voice stated.

"I'll be fine," Gavin told them, pushing them away. "I'll warm up by the fire." To his annoyance, he could barely walk, so Padriag helped him to sit in front of the fire and threw a thick blanket over his shoulders.

Gavin didn't have to ask why the two rushed from the room. They went to see about Liam.

Staring at the flames, Gavin fought falling asleep, an after effect of prolonged exposure to the cold. His eyes fluttered close and immediately pictures of his capture assaulted him. He gasped for air, feeling like a fish out of water and forced his eyes to remain open.

A long while later, Padriag returned. "Dude, you don't look too good," Padriag studied him. "I'll get you something hot to drink."

He returned quickly with a goblet and Gavin took it. He drank greedily from the hot liquid only to realize it had some sort of harsh taste. Surely one of Naill's tonics

Sputtering and choking as he tried to swallow, Gavin glared at the young knight. Padriag smiled. "To help you warm up." He waved a hand and the blanket wrapped tightly around Gavin.

"Loosen this blanket," Gavin gritted out.

"Nope." Padriag sat on a chair, eyebrows raised. "Niall said you needed to get warmed up."

Gavin struggled but realized it was useless. His arms pinned to his sides, he gave up. Admittedly, warmth was beginning to seep through. "How long since you returned with Liam?"

"About half a day."

"How does he fare?"

Padriag shrugged. "Not too bad from what I can see, most of his punishment was lashings."

Padriag's nonchalance revealed that, like the others, he'd been subject to lashings himself.

"Liam probably told Meliot not to mess up his hair." Laughing at his own joke, the young knight stood to refill the goblet. "I'm getting you a second drink. Your color's coming back."

"I don't want a damn drink." He wanted to be set free from the blanket so he could try to leap to Scotland. The sooner he could get out of this nightmare, the sooner he could help Tristan release them all from Meliot's clutches. "Get this accursed blanket off me. I must leave."

"Nope." Padriag held the goblet aloft. "Open up."

After struggling to get loose, he gave up as his arms and legs were tightly wrapped making it impossible to free himself. Finally, he did as the knight requested, needing to feel warmer and more drink was poured down his throat. When he choked, Padriag frowned. "Oops, sorry."

Gavin didn't bother glaring at him this time. "Can you at least get me clean clothing so that as soon as Niall returns, I can change and leave?"

"Nope." Padriag remained, the smile on his face showing that he enjoyed Gavin's frustration.

"When I get loose, I will slam you against every wall," he told the fool, his voice low. Padriag's smile faded.

"Alright, jeez. I sure do miss Tristan. At least he had a sense of humor."

IN A CHAIR by the large panoramic windows in the sitting room, book in her lap, the enchantress was reading. Sabrina's fiery hair seemed to glow from the sun coming through the glass.

Glad to have landed quietly this time, just outside the room, Gavin had the rare opportunity to study her. Her heart-shaped face looked serious, her brows furrowed at what she read. With an elbow on the armrest and head bent, she cupped her chin in her right hand. She sat with one leg folded under the other, a pink-nailed foot tapping impatiently on the floor.

She must have felt his presence because her pleased expression when she looked up didn't register surprise.

"Goldie, you're back." Her smile and sparkling hazel eyes caught him off guard and he couldn't help but smile back.

"Aye, I apologize for the taking so long. There was a...delay." He looked around the empty room. "Where are Tristan and Gwyneth?"

"They went to a meet someone in Edinburgh about estate business...er matters." She motioned to a chair. "Would you like some tea?"

He shook his head and sat.

The way she studied him made him feel as if she could see what he'd been through, the reminders of a distant past that had scarred him to the point Gavin doubted he could ever enjoy the pleasure of intimacy again. He didn't know her powers but hoped she could not read minds.

He looked past her to the window, spotting birds flying outside.

"You seem different," Sabrina told him, twirling a strand of hair between her fingers. "What happened?"

He didn't reply, couldn't reply, for a few moments collecting his thoughts. "Meliot took Liam, we had to fight to get him."

"Is he okay?"

He nodded.

"Look," Sabrina said, "Tristan and I had a long talk, about you." His stomach plummeted at her words. How much did Tristan reveal? Raising an eyebrow, he gave her an indifferent look.

"What did you discuss?"

"The terms of breaking your enchantment, for one. He suggested you and I build trust, that you have past experiences that could cause you to react badly if I try to make love with you."

She gave him a flirty smile, looking at him from under long lashes. "Maybe you are a man who needs to remain in control."

When she bit her bottom lip, he could not drag his eyes away, mesmerized, waiting for her to release the plump morsel. When she did, it was moist, and something in him stirred. It was a foreign, but welcome feeling.

"So," she continued getting his attention again. "I was reading this." She picked up a book and showed it to him. "It's the Kama Sutra, depicts all kinds of sexual positions. I'm thinking we can find one in here that will work."

Not used to such boldness from a woman, he was unable to stop his mouth from falling open and the rush of heat from surging up to his face. Feeling like a maiden, he cleared his throat trying to control his discomfort. "Er... Aye."

"Oh shit, I'm sorry. I keep forgetting you're from another time. Let me get you a drink of water...how can I be so stupid, sometimes I don't know why I'm the one that's here, not another woman. Although most women nowadays are just as open about sex as I am, to be fair."

Sabrina rushed from the room, still rambling. The book slid from the chair, landing on the floor, open. When she walked back in, he'd cocked his head to the side, likely trying to figure out what the people on the pages were doing.

She rushed to the book and grabbed it, closed it, then placed it on a table.

"Here. Please drink this." She held out a glass with amber-colored liquid in it. He took it and sniffed at it. "It's called sweet tea. We drink it every day, all day long in Georgia." Sitting down next to him on the couch, she tucked her foot under her bottom and waited for him to drink.

The combination of tea and lemon flavor was good. "It is very good, I like it. Thank you." He found himself entranced by her bright smile.

"Okay, so let's start over. How about this." She reached and took his hand in hers.

He reversed the hold, taking hers in his. "I'm not a lad, Sabrina, to be careful with." The dubious look she gave him angered him. "I'm a braw man, a head over six foot, five and thirty, when I left. No need to treat me as if I were a babe."

"Right," She snatched her hand out of his, rolling her eyes. "Well, help me here Goldie, what the hell are we supposed to do? We can try the spell, but if your big manly braw self is going to freak out when I try to fuck you, then it will be a waste of time—definitely a waste of mine." Crossing her arms, her eyes flashed impatiently at him.

"Fuck?"

"Oh shut up, I'm not going to translate. It's an old word.

You can always ask Padraig. Tristan says he speaks modern English."

"I know what fuck is. I am merely curious why you wish to fuck and not make love."

Her dainty huff made him smile. He drank the last of the cold tea and stood up, placing the glass down, he held his hand out to her.

"What are you doing?" She narrowed her eyes at him.

He didn't reply just lifted an eyebrow, getting his point across.

She took his hand and stood. He pulled her closer and held her against him. Sabrina looked up at him puzzled, but then shrugged and lay her head on his chest. They remained like that for a long while, neither moving.

"Can I put my arms around you?" she asked.

Tensing, he nodded. She moved gently, not timidly, but more as if she enjoyed the sensation of him. When her arms were completely around him, she merely linked her fingers, holding her hands in the small of his back, not moving. Closing his eyes, he inhaled the flowery perfume of her hair and relaxed.

At the sound of her sigh, he sighed too.

Bright colors suddenly flashed in his mind. Red. Dark ruby red. An angry slash of gold cut through the red background, before the smell of incense assaulted him. Gavin jumped away from Sabrina, his heart beating so hard he wondered if he would die.

"What is it?" She seemed to know better than to come closer, as she stayed still, just her hands reaching out. "Gavin?"

The room began to spin. He couldn't fight the pull back. How was he supposed to get closer toward freedom when it was impossible to remain longer than a few minutes?

"Gavin." Sabrina's annoyed utterance was the last thing he heard.

"Damn it." Sabrina stomped back to the couch. How were they going to work on the spell and curse, when the man kept disappearing?

She picked up the Kama Sutra and studied a picture, thinking of the look on Gavin's face when she'd showed it to him.

What a contradiction he was. The huge, tall and muscular warrior who faced mortal enemies on the battlefield, frightened of being touched the wrong way by her. He'd looked away from the pages when she'd returned with his drink, pretending interest in a flower vase.

Stretching out on the couch, she stared up at the ceiling. This thing between her and Gavin was moving much too slow. She'd planned to summon him to the Campbell estate, but he'd appeared before she'd set things up.

He'd felt so good in her arms. The way he'd sighed, almost as if, for a moment, he moved past whatever it was that scared him.

In that moment, holding him, it was as if no one else existed. She was beginning to develop feelings for Gavin. That couldn't be good.

Of course she felt for him. He was a good person. It wasn't just attraction, she felt, but a longing to see him free.

No one deserved the punishment the knights endured. Hundreds of years of imprisonment, constantly fighting for their lives, all because of a single act of heroism.

If she ever came face to face with the wizard, Meliot, she'd give him a piece of her mind. How a being could thrive on so much hatred was beyond her understanding. Probably a minion of the devil, because only someone influenced by darkness could hate so much.

The punishment was spurred when Gavin, Tristan and the other men had happened upon a village being attacked by Meliot's soulless warriors and they'd saved women Meliot had planned to use as personal incubators. So, he'd been denied the chance to spawn a bunch of children. How egotistical of the wizard to want to raise mini-me's to take over the world. It sounded like a plot for a very bad B-rated movie. She could see him being mad that his evil plans were dashed, but holding a grudge for almost four hundred years? That was just ridiculous.

Now the chance to break the curse was coming to an end. The four men in the alter-world didn't have a lot of time. In two years the men remaining in the alter-world would be trapped forever.

According to Tristan, they'd made a pact that they'd kill themselves before staying there, trapped for eternity.

Gavin would be free, she vowed. She'd do whatever had to be done to free him.

She'd set things up at the Campbell estate and summon him there. Perhaps being there would be helpful.

Heading to the guestroom, she made up her mind. She'd go back to Campbell Castle, summon him and move things along. The sooner he trusted her, the faster she could help him escape the enchantment.

Once all was done, she'd return to Atlanta and put all this behind her.

The thought of leaving Scotland gave her pause. She peered out a hallway window. The sun filtered through tall trees, rays reaching down to the lavish plantings in the back garden. Scotland was a beautiful, magical place.

To her shock, Sabrina realized she was already in love. Scotland had won her heart.

CHAPTER EIGHT

Liam's eyes fluttered open, noticed Gavin and then narrowed, hostile. Gavin leaned forward in the chair returning the look. He'd been there for hours, his turn to watch over the injured man. Liam hadn't been in danger of death, his recovery almost complete. Nonetheless, at times like these, the men always kept a close watch on each other. A sick man was a vulnerability.

"I've died and gone to hell," Liam's hoarse voice told of hours of screaming. "Get the fuck out of my room."

"And be denied the pleasure of your cantankerous presence? I think not." Gavin replied without rancor. He didn't dislike Liam, truth be told. The reason for their open hostility toward each other had never been spoken of out loud. He wondered if Liam held on to the resentment as a way to keep other things at bay.

He'd seen the panic in Liam's face upon wakening, fear that being freed from torment was no more than a dream. A feeling Gavin faced almost every morning for many years, so he understood.

"Go away. I do not need to be watched over." Liam tried to rollover, grunted and stopped. "Where's Niall?"

"He's done all he can," Gavin replied. "Your hip was crushed, it will take some time to heal fully. You cannot walk."

"How long?"

Gavin shrugged. "Days." They healed quickly in the alter-world, but even there a fracture like Liam's would take time. "Padriag will relieve me shortly. He will bring food. Need help relieving yourself?"

Liam's mouth fell open, closing only to open again.

"No." He turned away and held out a hand. "Hand me a basin and go away."

Gavin did as he'd asked, then turned his back allowing the man privacy, trying not to react to the soft groans. Even the slightest movement hurt Liam.

Unable to ignore Liam's pitiful sounds any longer, Gavin swung back around, aiding a red-faced Liam, who averted his eyes looking over Gavin's shoulder as he relieved himself. When Gavin helped him lay back on the bed, Liam was pale from the exertion.

Gavin emptied the pan and placed it back under the bed.

"I don't hate you Liam." Gavin wanted to clear things between them. If he left, there was a chance he'd never see the Englishman again. They'd been together too many years not to at least discuss the reasoning behind their animosity.

Liam merely grunted in response.

"You don't understand..."

"What?" Liam's response was almost a shout. "You know you are on the brink of leaving so you want to make amends now?

"We need to make things right between us."

Liam's upper lip curled. "Well, I hate you. That will not change. We have fought for many years, so the list of reasons is a long one."

The words slashed through Gavin.

There was only one real reason, but Liam stubbornly acted as if it had never happened. Gavin had hurt the man deeply, but there was nothing to be done about it. He could not change.

"Just know that you, like Niall and Padriag, are like a brother to me. I admit—I've never been a good friend to you Liam. For that I am sorry, but you make it very hard."

Liam sneered, "We will never be friends. Let us leave it at that."

"No, we must speak about it. That day, you and I were arguing and then fought. Suddenly things changed. One moment you hovered over me angry, the next you kissed me."

Liam went stock still.

"Understand that my reaction had more to do with my past. I didn't expect it. I am sure you didn't either. I detest my actions, how I reacted. It pains me to recall it."

"You are pained? As the one who was slammed against the wall, and told how despicable a human being I was, I cannot find it in me to be sad for you."

Gavin stood and moved to the doorway. "I am sorry."

Padriag walked in whistling, with a tray laden with food.

"Get out of my sight." Liam's hatred filled eyes met his. "Do not come back."

"Well I see you two are getting along as well as usual," Padriag said, putting the tray down next to Liam's bed. "Good morning, Liam."

"Leave, Padriag. I want to be alone."

"Nope."

PIERCING PAIN WOKE Liam from a deep sleep. Groaning, he waited for the throbbing to stop. He refused to allow Niall to heal him anymore. The man had practically collapsed after the last time. It was becoming too much for Niall, and he could move with a bit more ease. It was becoming bearable.

Anger surged at the memory of his earlier conversation. Gavin had apologized after almost four hundred years of animosity, with a shallow excuse. In truth, Liam hated the reminders that surrounded Gavin.

The kiss was forever etched in his mind. For so long Liam had fought the deep feelings for Gavin and had taken solace in being near him, seeing him daily.

That one time, when they'd fallen and he'd landed atop of Gavin, they'd frozen in place, neither moving. Nearness of any kind was something all of them missed, and in that moment, Liam was sure it wasn't just him who'd been caught unprepared for such intimate proximity.

In that moment, he had to know if there was a chance Gavin felt something for him. He couldn't resist it if his life had depended on it. All reason gone, he'd kissed Gavin fully on the lips.

Gavin had turned into stone, proving to Liam it had been a horrible mistake.

Face contorted in blind fury, Gavin had beaten him until the others heard and came to tear them apart. The pain of the bodily injuries was nothing compared to the breaking of his heart.

The only refuge, the only way to protect himself was to use anger, animosity and rage. Otherwise, Liam knew he would crumble.

Now on the brink of leaving, Gavin offered a truce. Asked for forgiveness. True, he'd apologized several times until becoming tired of Liam rebuffing with insults.

He could not forgive him. To do so would mean he accepted that Gavin was repulsed by him on a level different than their open animosity.

The door opened and Padriag tiptoed in only to yelp when his shin hit the corner of the bed.

"Shit, that hurt." The younger man limped around, setting a teapot down next to the bed. His eyes widened at seeing Liam awake.

"Hey, what are you doing awake?"

"The daggers in my hips woke me."

"Niall probably won't be up for another couple of hours, so I made you some special brew." Padriag poured the steaming liquid. His eyes flickered to the door.

Gavin walked in. "How is he?"

"Get the fuck out." Liam replied.

"He's awake, seems to be doing good," Padriag said. "What are you doing up?"

"Couldn't sleep," the Scot peered down at Liam. "I saw the light and wanted to tell someone I am going again."

Liam glared at him, not replying.

Padriag perked up, "Wait, I'll go with you to ensure the area is safe before you leap. Just gotta give Liam his medicine." Lifting Liam's head, the knight helped him drink. Almost immediately, the herbs soothed the pain and his eyelids became heavy.

Chapter Nine

The chill of the mist gave Castle Campbell a mystic appearance. The ruined castle loomed over the hillside, it's huge gates both a beacon and a warning. Once called Castle Gloom, today it earned its name.

Gavin's boots sunk into the damp moss with each step he took toward the structure he once called home.

Hundreds of years ago he had lived there, and the place was filled with the memories of his family, a time both rich in love and overflowing with reminders of what could have been.

Reaching the lower garden level, he turned, scanning the hillside, remembering how he and his brothers played in those woods, learned to hunt, fight, even have sexual encounters, when they could entice a local lass. Then he was taken, and everything changed.

Everyone he knew was long gone. There would never again be anyone to welcome him. The current clan chief lived near there, probably a distant descendant. In his heart, Gavin new he would never return to live here.

As he looked about, he realized that if indeed his enchantment ended, he did not have any resources.. Although still large, the Campbell's didn't plan for his return. The only reminder of his existence was an empty grave marked with his name date of birth and date he'd been dragged to the alterworld.

Sitting on a short wall, he pondered, as he'd often done over the years, how he'd earn his keep upon gaining freedom.

Tristan once told him he'd saved gold for all of them. Gavin would accept it as a loan if need be. Perhaps he'd discuss his limited options with Sabrina.

As if conjured, Sabrina stepped out of a small building. Fastening her coat, she glanced up and looked directly at him. Her face brightened. She gave him a wave then another hand signal he took to mean to stay and wait for her.

Gavin waved in return, startled at the erratic jolt in his chest. He understood why she'd summoned him here, however the castle was now a common stop for travelers to visit. It did not afford any privacy. Perhaps she'd found something helpful here.

"Hello Goldie." Her breathless greeting was accompanied with a friendly hug. "I'm so relieved I didn't have to hang around here waiting for days."

She held her hand out. "Come. I want you to tell me about this place."

He took her hand feeling somewhat uneasy. Not at holding her hand, but to walk as such, not something he was used to. Surprisingly, her small hand was like an anchor, and he found himself hoping she didn't pull it away.

"The castle and grounds are closed on Mondays and Tuesdays. I told the historical society I needed to scout it out for a photo shoot, and they agreed to let us walk around the grounds. If the guard asks, you're a model." She pulled him to a side garden. Finding a bench, they sat.

"What is a model? What skills would I possess if I were to be a model?"

Sabrina laughed shaking her head. "Models are people who earn a living posing for portraits, of sorts." She stood in a strange way holding one arm across her body and another beside her head. "I take photographs of men and women for merchants selling their wares. The models wear the clothing, jewelry or pretend to drive a car to promote...er show off the wares. A photograph is like a portrait." She pulled out a small flat item and showed it to him, a depiction of her on it.

"This is my license, it allows me to drive, um, manage a car on the road. This," she pointed at the depiction, "is my picture or photograph."

"I see," he nodded understanding that her image had somehow been captured. "Padriag told us about photos. I had not seen one."

She studied him. "Do you understand what a car is?"

"Aye," he nodded and pointed to several that were parked. "I have seen them over the years. I find them fascinating."

They walked for another hour, Gavin telling Sabrina about his life at the castle. The more he talked the easier it became, sharing his life with her. They returned to the small building she'd come out of earlier, and she turned her face up to him. "I have a surprise for you inside." She wiggled her finger at him, signaling for him to come closer. When he leaned forward, she kissed his jaw, and then opened the door.

THE APPREHENSION ETCHED on Gavin's face filled her with compassion. What had this man been through that totally robbed him of the ability to enjoy the company of a woman, not even trusting himself alone with one? He visibly relaxed after spotting the older man inside.

"Calum Campbell, at your service." The old man shook Gavin's hand, looking him over. "It is always a pleasure to have another Campbell on the grounds who dresses the part of our ancestors." He rounded the table and turned the book on it to face Gavin.

"Pictures of your ancestors and sketches of Castle Campbell as it once stood. A shame you were not here last month, the clan gathered for their annual reunion. Campbells from all over the world attend yearly."

Gavin studied the pictures as he flipped several pages. His brows pinched, a slight twitch at his jaw the only indication the knowledge that the people were his descendants affected him.

"I may recognize some of these people."

Mr. Campbell laughed. "I would think not young man, they haven't been alive for over a hundred years."

For a long time Gavin studied photographs and sketches of the keep, then he let out a breath. "There are few things that are wrong. The timbers for the gates were thicker..."

"Thank you Mr. Campbell," Sabrina cut in. "We appreciate your time, but Gavin's got jetlag. We'll return again when he's had rest." It was best to get him out of here before he began pointing out people in the drawings that he may have known.

The older man gave them a friendly smile. "Return anytime. I enjoy meeting Campbells."

Sabrina and Gavin walked out of the office, following a stone pathway to where cars were parked. When they reached her car, his face brightened. "I have seen these many times. I would like to ride upon it."

A man after her speed demon heart.

"Let's ride," she told him opening the passenger door.

The drive turned out to be the highlight of the day, Gavin studied her hands intently, asking questions about what she did with the pedals. He took great interest when she had to brake to avoid hitting a cow. Before long he was anticipating when she should slow down or speed up, remarking about it and sometimes even telling her to slow.

Normally she hated backseat drivers, but his comments amused her. Upon spotting a large, flat field she pulled over.

"Since you seem to know it all, why don't you give it a try. They switched seats and before long Gavin drove around the field with amazing ease. He pulled to a stop and asked how to turn the engine on and off. Then he took off again driving in straight lines, practicing reversing.

The pride in his face pulled at her heart. Who would have thought that the way to relax him would be driving lessons? Her only fear was that the man would disappear, and she'd be left with a driverless car headed for a tree.

"Ease into the road. This is a pretty remote area. Let's drive to the place I'm staying at tonight." Sabrina suggested, expecting him to say no. Instead, he smiled brightly and drove onto the road, taking them without incident all the way to the inn where she had reserved a room.

Thankfully, she'd thought ahead and had packed food, just in case he didn't disappear. They had lunch in the car parked near the inn as she didn't dare bring him around people as he was dressed rather out of style.

She sized him up. "Gavin, I'm going to buy you modern clothing and some sunglasses to cover your face, when you return, hopefully you can linger for a longer time. What do you think?"

The sunlight reflected off his golden hair, his amber eyes especially light. "Aye, I would like that. I would like to drive again too."

"I'm surprised you've remained so long this time," she told him watching him empty his water bottle.

"Me as well."

"No pull back yet?"

"Not yet, but I expect it any time."

She began putting their discarded napkins and sandwich wrappings back into a bag. "Would you like to see the inside of the Inn?"

Surprisingly, he didn't hesitate, but instead climbed out of the car and looked with expectancy towards the door of the Inn. "Aye."

They managed to skirt the front desk and go down the hall to where her room was without being seen.

Sabrina sat on the bed in the guestroom as Gavin used

the bathroom. Once inside, he'd asked if there was a place he could relieve himself and she felt bad for not thinking about it earlier.

"Thank you," Gavin said as he came back into the bedroom, his expression so happy, it made her feel the same. "I enjoyed myself today. It has been a long time since I did."

She stood, not risking touching him. "I'm glad." She pointed to the television in the corner. "Do you want to learn about televisions?"

"Nay." He stood so close that when he spoke his breath warmed the side of her face. She turned slowly, not daring to hope that he would finally kiss her.

Tentative hands cupped her face, his eyes locked on her lips. When he finally did lean forward and touch his lips to hers, those beautiful amber eyes fell closed. The kiss, timid at first, began to deepen. He turned his face sideways his mouth demanding. At first she resisted every instinct to touch him, but when his tongue moved into her mouth, she placed her hands on his shoulders to keep from crashing into him.

His taste was the unique flavor of a man. His soft hair fell forward brushing her face and Sabrina inhaled the smell of outdoors and musk. Wonderful.

His hands traveled down her back, when finally he cupped her bottom pulling her into his hardness, she moaned in relief. His lips began to travel ever so slowly down the side of her neck, his breathing fast.

Gavin straightened, his now-dark amber eyes meeting hers. "Ye are an amazing woman, Sabrina." He frowned slightly. "I should go."

"Should?" She was not letting him off the hook that easy.

"You said 'should', not must. So you don't feel the pull yet do you?"

He didn't answer, his gaze flickering to the bed. "I do not."

The connection between them was tangible, a strong tension that reflected in his gaze. He felt it as much as she did. He wanted her as much as she wanted him. True, it wouldn't be making love, but sex with him would be a good start. That was if they made it that far.

Remembering what Tristan had stated—that he had to be in control otherwise it could prove dangerous—Sabrina lowered her shoulders and took in the sight of him.

"Just watch me. I am not expecting anything," Sabrina said moving closer to the bed.

Sabrina drew her blouse off slowly, her green eyes locked with his. Pulling the zipper down on her jeans, she slid them off, stepping out of them. She unclasped her bra and allowed it to drop, not once breaking eye contact. His breathing became labored, and he didn't look away, the darkened amber gaze traveling over her body. Smiling now at his obvious interest, she slipped her panties off.

Naked, she lifted her arms over her head and turned in a circle. "Like what you see Goldie?" Hoping that making light would help ease some of the tension, Sabrina wiggled her butt. "Are you a butt guy or a boob guy?"

It worked because he huffed and gave her a droll look. "I like everything I see at this moment."

"I promise I will not touch you, Gavin, but you can touch me if you wish."

The serious expression returned and after just a moment's hesitation, he closed the distance between them.

Sabrina stood still, but relaxed. The fact she stood stark naked before a fully dressed Gavin was intoxicating. Her body tingled with desire and anticipation.

Expecting a touch or a kiss, she was surprised, when he pulled her close and kissed the top of her head. Perplexed, Sabrina kept her arms down at her sides, unsure of what to do.

Then she felt it, a slight shiver, as if he was cold. Gavin ran his hands down her back, taking his time. The timid touch made Sabrina want to squirm. Instead, she let out a slow breath and lifted her face.

His eyes bored into hers. "You are so beautiful, you deserve a man who is not broken."

"Will you kiss me?" Sabrina asked, ignoring the last part of his comment. "Because I want you. Only you."

There was a flicker of indecision in his eyes before he pressed his lips to hers. The kiss wasn't deep, but strangely passionate. There was no mistaking the desire, the want and need.

When he deepened the kiss, his hands shook as he ran them over her bare skin. "I wish I could bury myself deep in you. I want to be able to sink into your body and claim you as mine." His husky words made her tremble with desire.

"You will do it. We will break your curse."

His arms dropped and he let out a shaky breath. There was a light sheen over his face and recognizing the moment of connection between them was broken, Sabrina stepped back and grabbed her blouse, pulling it on over her head. It hung just below her butt.

"What are you not telling me?" She crossed her arms. "I am working my ass off here to help you. If you keep secrets, how fair is that to me and the others?"

He hung his head, and just when she thought he'd not speak, he did. "Even before the curse I could not be with a woman. Because...of what happened to me in the past.

Shame draped over him like a thick wet cloak. "I...I was kept as a..." He closed his eyes and let out a slow breath, his entire body rigid. Sabrina wanted to stop him to tell him he didn't have to tell her everything. His freedom demanded that she know every detail and it cut her to the core that he had to divulge his darkest secret.

His amber eyes opened, and he looked straight into hers. "I was a sex slave."

His demeanor changed before Sabrina's eyes. By the rounding of his shoulders and keeping his eyes averted, he expected revulsion, rejection.

She could not only see the pain, but almost feel it as it was so tangible. Not only did her heart break for him, but rage surged at how cruel humans could be.

"What happened to you is not your fault and nothing to be ashamed about. To this day, humans are being stolen and used in the sex trade. Gavin, I cannot begin to imagine what you went through, and I will not make light of it. Getting past it will be difficult, but not impossible. Look what just happened between us. I would call it progress, and it was nice."

There was a slight twitch to the corners of his lips. His

expression changed, to more relaxed, and he nodded. "I agree. I enjoyed it as well."

Sabrina shimmied moving her shoulders forward and back smiling up at him. "I know you did, Goldie."

He began to fade. "I must go now."

Sabrina hurried toward him and lifted her mouth. Just as their lips touched, he disappeared.

"Talking about being ghosted," Sabrina muttered flopping back onto the bed.

THE FOLLOWING DAY, back at Dunimarle Castle in Culross, Sabrina hurried into the house and straight up to the guestroom, not wanting to see anyone just yet. She climbed into the bed and stared up at the ceiling.

The night before in the room in the inn, she'd fallen asleep almost immediately after Gavin disappeared.

She'd not tell anyone what Gavin had disclosed, although she expected Tristan knew or had some idea. The poor guy had been through so much before the enchantment, he didn't need the added burden of others knowing his secret.

Just knowing what he'd endured gave her more reason to save him, to allow him the opportunity to have a normal life, whether it be with or without her. This was not the time to be selfish, not when there was someone like him, who deserved a better life so much more than many.

"Hey, what are you doing in bed? Are you sick?" Gwen loomed over her, reaching to touch her forehead. "I heard you come in about an hour ago."

Allowing her sister to check for a fever, Sabrina sighed. "I'm not sick, needed some time alone and didn't want my day ruined by running into Fiona."

"She's gone," Gwen said, a smile curving her lips. "I told her to leave after I caught her cozying up to Tristan." Hands on her hips and a frown on her brow, Gwen shook her head. "The nerve of that girl."

Sabrina sat up. "Eww, they're cousins. Albeit very distant centuries apart cousins, but still, she doesn't know that? What happened?" She knew Gwen needed to talk about it.

"I went to the stables to find Tristan just as that hussy walked up to him and slid a hand up his chest and told him he was hot. And then said it was a total turn on to do it in the stables." Gwen held up her finger to make air quotes. "Total turn on."

"She's a freak," Sabrina said and then grinned imagining Tristan's reaction. "What did Tristan do?"

"He was backing up, pushing her hands away and sputtering something about them being cousins." Gwen chuckled. "I think he was too stunned to speak clearly."

"Poor guy. So you came up and saved him then?"

Gwen nodded. "Told her she had half an hour to pack her shit before I'd begin chucking it into the trash."

"I wish I'd been there to see it," Sabrina said and then added. "I'm glad she's gone. It makes things easier with Gavin appearing and disappearing out of nowhere."

"I tell you what Sabrina, I don't envy you one bit." Gwen plopped down on the bed with a huff.

"What don't you envy?" Sabrina asked, perplexed.

"When you and Gavin get together, with his looks, you'll need to get a stick or a taser to keep women away."

Sabrina rolled her eyes, "You assume a great deal sister. He will be a free man. He may not want to be tied down as soon as he's free. I don't want him to stay with me out of gratitude."

She gave his looks some thought. "If he did, I'd buy him the biggest wraparound sunglasses I could find and make him grow a beard."

"What about that killer bod?"

"Baggy clothes and feed him lots of donuts."

They burst out laughing, until Gwen studied her.

"Did you do it?" Gwen asked. "Did you have sex with him, and not tell me. You have this strange look about you."

"No. Well, we kissed. I was naked. But nothing happened. It was an experiment." Sabrina hated that her cheeks burned.

"I knew it!" Gwen wiggled and clapped. "Details."

"We did not have sex," Sabrina insisted. "He has a lot to get past. I understand now why that evil Meliot gave him that obstacle. I won't divulge his past, unless necessary. Intimacy with him causes...issues."

She ran her hands down her face and gave Gwen a long look. "Shit what I can tell you is that there is a lot to get past."

"Wow, the situation seems very complicated," Gwen said slowly, covering her mouth with both hands. "What an asshole that wizard is. I can't imagine what happened to poor Gavin."

"You can ask Tristan. I'm sure he knows what Gavin would be willing to share," Sabrina uttered.

"I won't. I don't need to know such intimate details. If we feel that it's necessary to break the enchantment, then it should be Gavin who shares." Gwen stood and looked around the room as if searching for answers to so many unanswered questions. "So where did you leave things after visiting Keep Campbell?"

"I have to work on some kind of strong ward that will allow me to touch him and him to enjoy it without flashbacks or whatever the hell happens to him that causes it to be dangerous."

"What do you have to do?" Gwen gave her a worried look, her eyes narrow. "Do you have to do something dangerous?"

"Not exactly....okay fine." She gave up and told her sister.

"Whoever breaks the enchantment, must make love to him. And he has to relinquish himself totally without any hesitation. He has to allow someone...me...free access to his body, which would be extremely difficult for him. At least that's the gist I'm getting."

When she was done Gwen's eyebrows were raised high, her mouth forming an O.

"What are you going to do? The fact that he cannot be touched is what makes the curse hard to break." Gwen bit her bottom lip. "How to get around it. Lots of food for thought."

"You think?"

CHAPTER TEN

"Let's see if you can stand up," Padriag said sliding a hand under Liam's arm.

Niall did the same on the opposite side helping Liam up from the bed.

Stabbing sensations shot through his hips, but he managed to remain standing. He puffed out breaths waiting for the throbbing to subside. It did, just a bit.

"You can let go," he told them. Reluctantly, they released him. He wobbled and took a step. The pain was not as bad as the initial shock of standing.

Liam took several more tentative, excruciating steps. "You can stop hovering. I will not fall."

"There's our little ray of sunshine," Padriag said arms loosely at his sides, ready to catch him if he fell.

"Where is Gavin?" Liam asked, surprised the man wasn't around to pester him. Niall and Padriag exchanged glances, eyebrows raised. "Not that I care. I expected him to be here, just to annoy me."

"He's still on the other side," Padriag replied with a frown. "He should have returned by now."

"Aye," Niall agreed. "It is worrisome, unless his enchantment has been broken."

They waited all day and still Gavin did not appear. Several times Padriag went to the place where he'd appear, and he was not there.

When night came, they expected he would be there the following morning.

THE NEXT MORNING Liam could get out of bed unassisted with barely a twinge of pain. He went down the stairs cautiously, one hand bracing on to the wall. Niall and Padriag sat at the large table in the great room, in deep conversation. They didn't hear or see him enter.

"One of us has to try to go to Tristan's home," Padriag said. "At least to find out if Gavin's been broken free. If he's trapped by Meliot, then we can plan to go and rescue him. Although, I do not think he has returned here."

"What's happening?" Liam asked nearing the table.

"Gavin still has not returned," Padriag told him. "One of us has to go and try to find out what happened."

Liam closed his eyes concentrating on an image of Gavin, pulling in any foresight that came. He saw Gavin, lying on a wet surface, like stones. He was alive. There was a man bent over him.

"I'll go." He told them moving to the middle of the room.

"The door is that way," Padriag pointed at the front door.

"I can leap from within the keep."

"Now you tell us?" Padriag walked up to him, eyes narrowed. "What else are you not telling us?"

"Have a care," Niall warned, standing. The quiet man's eyes met Liam's. "Tell Tristan that Gavin was pulled back by Meliot prior to going to the real world, that he relived his past. It could be the reason for this delay."

Liam nodded, knowing it was useless to ask for more details. "I will return as soon as possible."

He leaped.

TRISTAN'S HOME was larger than Liam expected. A large grey stone edifice, with imposing gates and large rounded wooden doors looked every bit the sixteenth century keep. He stood in front of it, looking around to see a long drive and many trees. He inhaled the fresh air, allowing the memories of it to barely tickle, before heading for the front door.

He was shocked when Tristan himself opened the door, grabbing him into a bear hug. Seeing him brought feelings that Liam didn't expect, joy and the urge to cry.

"Liam, why are you here? Have you escaped the enchantment?"

"I am not free and unsure how long I can remain. Something happened."

Tristan kept his arm around Liam's shoulders as he ushered him into the home, yelling for Gwyneth to come.

Gwyneth rushed into the front room, behind her a redhead Liam assumed was Sabrina.

Gwyneth smiled broadly at him, her bright green eyes sparkling. "Liam!" She rushed forward and embraced him and then kissed his jaw. "How is this possible?"

"What happened to Gavin?" The husky female voice got his attention. The red-haired enchantress locked gazes with him. She was beautiful, with large, green eyes, a heart shaped face and pouty lips. The woman would make a good partner for Gavin, both being astonishingly attractive.

"Something's wrong isn't it?" She approached him, paling more with each step.

Liam nodded. "Gavin never returned to the alter-world. Is he not here?"

"No," Tristan said, worry emanating from him.

"Oh my God." Gwyneth went to her sister.

"Sit down Sabrina, you look about to faint."

Gwen's comment brought a glare from her sister. "I don't faint."

Tristan turned to him. "Liam are you sure he has not returned to the alter-world? You didn't sense his entrance?"

"Nay, none of us felt him reenter. He remains in this realm."

"Is that a terrible thing?" Sabrina asked, not allowing her sister to lead her to a chair.

Liam deferred to Tristan, who replied. "Aye. We cannot remain in this realm overly long. Until the enchantment is broken, we age quickly if we remain away for too long."

"How quickly?" Sabrina, her face reflecting the same fear he felt.

Liam shrugged. "Perhaps about a year for each day."

This time Sabrina did sink into a chair. Her legs must have given out because she seemed surprised to find herself sitting and she sprang up. "We have to find him. We need a plan."

"How old was he when he entered the enchantment?" Gwen asked, eyeing her sister.

"Five and thirty," Liam replied. "How many days since he left here?"

Both Tristan and Gwen looked at Sabrina. "He was here the day before last. When he vanished, and I assume he returned to your world."

Liam's stomach lurched.

Gwen met his gaze. "Do the days here or there count against you?"

"We believe here, but we've never had to test it. It is what we were told when first enchanted. Of course it could have been another of Meliot's many lies," Tristan said and then turned his attention to Sabrina. "Did he say anything prior to leaving? Did the pull for him to leap seem different?"

Sabrina nodded. "There was something different. For one thing, he stayed much longer than normal. At one point I asked if he felt the urge to return and he said no. Instead of the way he usually just disappears, this time he seemed to fade slowly."

"He's here, in this realm," Liam told them sensing Gavin was near. He studied Sabrina for a moment. The woman was hard to read. Although it was obvious she was fearful of what happened with Gavin, she was not distraught. Had yet to suggest magic to help.

Pushing his assessment aside, Liam described his vision to them. "I saw Gavin lying in wetness. It looked to be a cobblestone road."

"Can you try again and see if you can notice anything different?" Sabrina asked. This time he noted the worry lines. She was indeed distraught.

Closing his eyes, he held his hands palms up and allowed his mind to open to his power of foresight.

Slowly a picture formed. Gavin no longer lay in the wet ground. Instead, he seemed to be walking into some sort of bookstore. The vision was blurry, but he clearly saw words etched onto the glass of the door. "Stewart's," he whispered, then the vision was gone.

"Is there a bookstore near here called Stewart's?" he asked.

"You have to be kidding me?" Sabrina exclaimed, "This is freaking Stewartland!" She dashed to a desk and began pounding at the keys on a device. "I'm googling it. If we get less than five hundred hits, I'll be shocked."

"I'll make some phone calls, going to get my cell." Gwen rushed from the room, leaving Tristan and Liam standing, neither with a clue what to do.

"I'll call for Miles. He'll help," Tristan said, a triumphant look on his face as he hurried from the room.

Liam watched Sabrina as she glanced at the display on her device. Even with her brow scrunched with worry and lips pressed tight, she was astonishingly beautiful. Gavin had definitely met his match. He moved closer, not daring to speak, not sure it would affect what she studied.

Her gaze rose to his. "Thank you for coming, the sooner

we find him, the better." She held her hand out, after hesitating, he took it. She smiled at him. "You will be leaving the enchantment soon Liam. I sense it."

Astounded, he withdrew his hand. He liked her. That he had not expected.

She picked up a small device and pointed to it. "Telephone. It allows me to communicate with other people in other locations. I'm calling the first bookstore on the list."

She glanced back at the display. "Yes, hello. I'm looking for a friend of mine that went to your bookstore yesterday. He's about six-five, blonde, very good looking. You can't miss him...."

Gwen returned, another one of the same devices at her ear. She patted his shoulder in passing.

When Tristan returned a bearded older man of thick build, with solid gray hair, walked in with him. Instantly Liam could tell the man was someone of good character by the lack of judgement when the man met his eyes and nodded in greeting.

"Listen to me," Tristan said, getting Miles' attention. "I will explain something that may be hard for you to believe."

Liam sat, all the activity reassuring.

Gavin would not be missing for long. He avoided the thought that Gavin could be trapped there and age until dying.

CHAPTER ELEVEN

Cold drizzle pelting his face woke Gavin. He tried to sit up, but everything tilted, and he almost threw up. Moving slower, he once again lifted himself and looked around. Nothing looked familiar. Water dripped from his drenched hair, every movement making him so dizzy he had no choice but to lay back onto the wet ground.

"Sir, are you injured? Is there something I can get for you?" a male voice asked.

He opened his eyes to see two images meld into one. A man stood over him, peering down. He held a stick with circular item that kept more rain from falling on him. "I think we need to get you out of the rain. Come." He held his hand out, and Gavin took it, needing the man's strength to stand.

Strangely, once he stood, some of the dizziness evaporated. Not sure where he was, except for the fact that it was definitely not the alter-world, he followed the man into a shop, a bell cheerfully jingling over the door as they entered.

Once inside, he recognized it to be a book shop. There were shelves upon shelves against every wall, filled with carefully placed books. Along the center, oval shaped tables displayed more books and bottles that were filled with what looked to be herbs. Each bottle was labeled in neat handwriting.

The man who'd invited Gavin to follow him looked to be in his thirties, slight of build with dark hair. He led him to the back room, a parlor of sorts.

Still not introducing himself, the bespectacled brown eyes took Gavin in as the man removed his wet coat and hung it on a hook.

"I'll get you something dry so you can change out of those wet clothes. I will return shortly." With that, the man hurried from the room.

Unsure what to do and unable to sit since he was soaked, Gavin studied the surroundings. Moments later, the man returned holding clothing.

He seemed the friendly sort. "I'm John by the way, John Stewart." He handed him some grey clothing and pointed to a door. "All I have are these sweats. I ordered them the wrong size, I suppose it's a good thing, now. You can change in there, the bathroom is big enough."

John looked him over with curiosity. "We have much to discuss."

Pondering the man's words, Gavin went to the small room. Not sure what to do with his wet clothes, he removed them and piled them into a basin attached to the wall. Using a cloth, he dried himself before pulling on the soft clothing the man had given him. Instead of boots, the man had given him thick stockings.

Gavin found John in an adjoining room, a kitchen. He'd poured two cups of what he recognized as coffee and motioned for him to sit down. In the middle of the table, a plate laden with sweet biscuits tempted him.

"Please help yourself," John said smiling at him. "If you're hungry, I can make you a sandwich."

Gavin shook his head, unsure if he could eat or drink. Strangely, it felt as if he didn't belong, as if he should be elsewhere. "Thank you for the clothing. What place is this?"

"My book shop. We are in Edinburgh, Scotland," John replied. "What is your name?"

It was then he realized he did not know for sure. A name that felt somewhat familiar came to mind. "I believe my name is Gavin, Gavin Campbell."

"I see," John said, his expression blank. "Where do you come from? By your dress, it seems you're not from the twenty-first century."

Not sure what the man spoke about, Gavin cocked his head to the side. "I am not from here. I do not know or remember where I come from."

"Do you remember anything?"

Gavin didn't.

After a moment, he gave up and drank the coffee.

"Hold on. Let me get a book, Campbell." John got up and went to the front room. Gavin heard him moving things around and a thump when something fell, followed by a curse. It was a long moment before John returned. When he did, the man stopped in his tracks, his mouth falling open. "You, um, your beard and hair grew."

Gavin felt his face. He did need to shave, but he didn't understand John's reaction.

"When I left the room, you were almost clean shaven. Now you have more than a five o'clock shadow. Oh no." John's eyes widened, sending alarm bells through Gavin.

"What is wrong?"

John paced the room; removing his glasses he pinched his nose. "Something is very off. I wonder if you are out of your time. Perhaps a time traveler." John shook his head. "Is that even possible?"

The man paced, opening a book and turning the pages. "We have to find a way to return you where you belong and fast."

"Clan Campbell is huge, there are probably hundreds of Gavin Campbells in Scotland, if not thousands. Does Duke of Argyll ring a bell?"

It didn't.

"Come." Mumbling to himself, John motioned for him to follow, and they made their way back into the shop. Gavin watched as John began pulling books and flipping through pages.

Picking up the glass bottle, Gavin peered inside. "Are you a wizard?"

John glanced up at him his brows drawing together. "Er, yeah, well sort of. More of a witch. This is most peculiar. What year are you from?"

Gavin shrugged. "I lived in Scotland in the sixteen hundreds. At least that is what I think." He looked around the space. "Is this your shop?"

The man nodded while flipping pages anew. "Yes. I live upstairs. There are two bedrooms and bathroom above." He said, pointing to the ceiling.

"Please sit," John studied an open book and began putting different items into a large black bowl. Gavin stopped watching after a while and went to stand by the front window. The rain stopped, but the day remained overcast. Occasionally a means of transportation went by. A flicker of a memory formed, him riding one such vehicle. It caught him by surprise, but as quick as it came, it was gone. Seeing a woman crossing the street, he watched her until she turned a corner and was no longer visible. Did he have a woman in his life? Why didn't he remember anything?

"Do you have a wife?" He asked John, not turning away from the window.

"Oh, no, I am not married. I don't...er..." John left off, and sneezed, "Oh goodness, these ingredients sure do smell. Open the window please."

The fresh air cooled the room immediately, and Gavin went back to watch John. Closing his eyes, he tried to remember things, but it only brought a pounding to his temples, almost as if something was intent on keeping him from remembering. Still he pushed through, hoping for any detail, no matter how small.

John looked at him for a moment then away, seeming nervous, uneasy around him. Yet, the man's presence gave Gavin ease. It was as if they were meant to be friends, or at least acquaintances. A picture of a blond man formed, but he couldn't place the face with the memory.

"Okay. Sit down, let me light these candles and we'll begin." John lit a candle; it flickered weakly and went out. "Damn it." John hurried to the open window and closed it. He relit the candles. This time they remained ignited, and John sat across from Gavin.

He poured liquid into the concoction in the bowl and began stirring it, chanting a spell. Words in a language Gavin did not understand.

When John opened his eyes, Gavin waited. "Close your eyes, tell me what you see."

Gavin closed his eyes. An image of a woman formed in his mind, fair of skin, she stood nude next a bed. She was exquisite. Was this his wife? His eyes flew open. "I may be married."

John's eyes went to his left hand. "You're not wearing a ring, but it's possible. What did you see?"

"A woman, red hair, beautiful."

"Did a name come to you?"

Gavin concentrated. "Liam."

"Um, that's a man's name. Who is Liam?"

"I do not know."

John frowned. "All right, let's concentrate on the woman. Close your eyes again." He began chanting once more. Gavin did his best to concentrate on the image of the woman he'd seen. This time he saw her smiling broadly at him. They were outdoors. She waved and began walking towards him. He concentrated on the memory and saw her sitting next to him, showing him a small item with a depiction of her face on it.

"Sabrina. Her name is Sabrina," he told the wide-eyed John.

"Sabrina Lockhart."

CHAPTER TWELVE

The sitting room at the McRainey estate was abuzz with activity. Gwen, Sabrina, and even Tristan, all with cell phones to their ear, calling every Stewart bookstore in Scotland and England.

Miles, the estate foreman, had instructed Tristan on how to dial and talk into a cell phone when Tristan had first been freed. Sabrina's heart pitched at how hard everyone worked to find Gavin.

Not wanting to think about the sun setting and day one beginning, she hurriedly drew lines through a phone number she'd already called and dialed the next number on the page. Not even halfway down the page, she wondered how many more were left.

A gruff voice answered, and she began her spiel, "I am looking for a friend that may have some to your bookstore....No sir, I don't know what your bookstore hours are... Yes sir, I am aware of the time. Can you tell me if a tall blond, handsome man came to your store today....Yes sir, I know you're closed but can you please just...." The man hung up and she stared at the phone, incredulous at his rudeness.

Tristan frowned, nodding his head, "Aye, that's right. I am in search of a friend who may have visited your bookshop."

"Oh boy," Sabrina sighed, giving Gwen a pointed look, who leaned toward Tristan and coached him on what to say.

An incoming call caught her by surprise. It was an unknown number, and she almost didn't answer, but she didn't want to take any chances. Perhaps one of the people at book shops she'd called earlier remembered something.

"Hello?"

"May I speak to Sabrina Lockhart?" The male's voice sounded hesitant. It was followed by a sneeze. "Sorry."

"How can I help you?" Sabrina waited for the sales pitch so she could hang up.

"Well you see, My name is John Stewart, I own a bookstore in Edinburgh."

Sabrina stood and waved her arms to signal the others, putting the phone on speaker.

"Yes, please continue."

"I FOUND a man outside in the rain, he says his name is Gavin Campbell. He is here in my shop with me and remembered your name, but nothing more. Do you know him?"

"Oh God, yes!" Sabrina cried out, looking at everyone who'd gathered close, listening intently. "Is Gavin there now, in your bookstore?" She wiped an errant tear away. "Can you put him on the phone please?"

"One minute," the man replied. She heard John instructing Gavin to speak into the phone, then telling Gavin she was on the line and would hear him if she spoke. Finally Gavin's voice sounded.

"Are you there?"

"Gavin, yes, are you alright?" Everyone held their breath awaiting her next words.

"Aye, I am well. I do not remember how I came to be here." Gavin sounded confused and she figured he had a hard time understanding the mechanics of a telephone.

"We are not far, perhaps an hour away. Remain there with John, do not go anywhere with anyone. Do you understand?"

"Aye," he replied.

"Gavin, this is Tristan...Tristan...Aye, I am your friend. Can you leap?" Tristan leaned over the phone, his brow furrowed as he spoke. "Can you not return to the alter-world?"

"I do not understand," Gavin replied, sounding hesitant.

Gavin continued talking. "I do not remember you or anyone, just Sabrina...is she my wife?"

The floor swayed under her feet, and she reached to the desk for support. "Gavin, this is Sabrina. Listen, I'll be there as soon as possible, you need to get some rest alright? Can you give the phone back to John?"

"Hello?" John answered.

"What happened to him?" Sabrina asked. "He doesn't remember anything."

"That's correct, he doesn't seem to. I was coming home from the bakery up the street. He was outside, on the sidewalk. I thought he'd passed out or something, so I checked, and his style of dress caught my attention. When he began speaking old English, I decided to bring him here to the shop. He is not from our time is he?"

How could the man possibly guess this? There was something about his voice that eased her, the slight hesitation at asking. Her gut clenching, she decided to be truthful. "No, he isn't. We have to help him return to his own place. It's imperative."

"He's aging," John told her, his voice quiet, probably didn't want Gavin to hear. "His beard is growing, but he doesn't look too different from what I can tell."

Sabrina and John spoke a bit longer. She asked him several times to assure her he'd keep an eye on Gavin and confirmed his address.

"Hurry, go," Miles told them. "I will remain here in case any of the other men reappear."

"I will drive," Sabrina said hurrying from the room. "First a coat and my bag."

Chapter Thirteen

The room above the bookshop had a low ceiling. Gavin ducked into the bathroom to take a shower. The rush of hot water washed over him, and he closed his eyes enjoying the unusual sensation.

After speaking to Sabrina and the man, Tristan, John insisted he go upstairs and rest. Not sure what else to do, he tried to sleep, but after an hour of lying in bed and not falling asleep, he got up and tinkered with the fixtures until he figured out how to get the water to spill out.

Although not sure about anything, something urgent seemed to pull at him. A strange feeling like that of falling sideways came and went.

Once out of the shower, he dried and once again pulled on the clothes John had loaned him, then went to the window and peered out at the road below. The night was bright, lit by flameless torches standing every few feet. A lone figure stood below one, not moving, huddled against the night coolness.

Gavin looked closer, but could not make out the person's features, other than a grey beard. It seemed as if the person stared up at his window. A rush of wind blew the man's hood off, and his stark grey hair blew in the wind. A sneer formed on the man's lips. Pale hands pulled the hood back up. The man was familiar. Gavin stepped away from the window, uneasiness creeping up his spine.

The woman, Sabrina, had assured him that she and the man called Tristan would arrive soon. For some reason, he knew that, with her arrival, he'd be more at ease. The woman was very important to him, of that he was sure.

The conversation with Tristan confused him. The man insisted he leap and will himself to another location. His familiar tone told Gavin they knew each other well, and the cadence of Tristan's speech was very much like his own. The idea of leaping or willing himself to another location did not make sense.

Hopefully once the others arrived, answers would come. When he peered out the window again, the old man was gone.

GWEN HAD INSISTED on driving claiming Sabrina was much too nervous and should be spending her time researching.

As they arrived at the outskirts of Edinburgh, still without any answers as to what could have possibly happened to Gavin, Sabrina became more and more restless, tapping her fingers on the armrest and every few minutes glancing at her watch.

Very soon another day would pass, and Gavin would age another year. Grateful that no one spoke to her, she allowed her thoughts free rein. How would they convince Gavin to leap back to the alter-world? If he couldn't remember anything, it would be difficult.

About to ask Tristan his thoughts, she changed her mind, seeing the large warrior's death grip on his arm rest. She decided to divert his attention. "Tristan, has this happened before? Have any of you lost their memory?"

"No, never. It must be Meliot's doing. To keep him from breaking his curse."

"If he can't remember anything, he may not be able to do it," Sabrina said.

Tristan's worried eyes met hers. "I have considered that. Perhaps we can try to summon one of the others to appear and take him back."

"Perhaps Liam. He is the one who came to inform us Gavin was missing. It could be that he can appear in different locations."

She bit her bottom lip thinking. "If Meliot meant to hide Gavin from us to keep from breaking the spell, why did he keep him so close?"

The knight shook his head. "I do not know. I suspect Meliot has little control in this realm."

"That makes sense I suppose," Sabrina replied glancing at her watch again. How much longer before we get there?

"Shouldn't be too much longer," Gwen replied looking at the GPS. "Perhaps a half hour."

Exactly twenty-five minutes later, Gwen pulled over in front of the non-descript book shop. "I will park. Go inside."

Sabrina and Tristan got out and hurried towards the bookshop's front door. An old-fashioned shingle sign hung over the door. "Stewart Books & Magic."

The lights were on, giving them a clear view of a man who opened the front door. Sabrina suspected it was John Stewart.

He had kind brown eyes and a look of relief as he moved back, allowing them in.

"Hello, I am John. I assume you are Sabrina and Tristan, was it?"

Both she and Tristan nodded as he continued with barely a pause.

"I'm so glad you're here. He went upstairs right after I spoke with you, but I heard him up and about. I am sure he's too confused to rest."

He led them through the booklined room and on to a stairwell next to what looked to be a sitting room.

"I'll go see him first, then I'll call for you," she told Tristan, who nodded understanding. On the way there, they'd discussed not wishing to overwhelm Gavin. They would take their time with him in hopes his memories would return.

The stairs creaked under her feet as she climbed the narrow stairway. Spotting the first doorway, she peeked inside.

At the sight of Gavin sitting on the bed, tears sprang to her eyes. He looked up and stood at seeing her. The short beard made him appear older, but, leaning closer to inspect him, she didn't see any other signs of aging. Not yet.

He seemed confused for a moment, before his eyes widened and he smiled at her. Something fluttered in her stomach, but she pushed it away. This was not the time for silly things.

"Ye came. Are ye taking me home?" he asked, studying her.

Sabrina nodded, "I'm going to try."

He caught her by surprise, wrapping his arms around her and pulling her against him, his mouth seeking hers. The man acted very familiar for someone who didn't remember her.

Sabrina kissed him back, taking advantage of the fact that his lack of memory must have erased his past experiences along with the inhibitions.

Albeit reluctantly, she pushed back from him. "Gavin, there are others downstairs, waiting to see you."

"Are ye my wife?" The heat in the amber eyes sent shivers through her. If only some of his memories would stay away forever.

"Not quite," she replied, not sure what to say about their relationship at this point. "We are friends."

A pensive expression formed. "We will marry."

"Why do you say that?"

"I must love ye. How could I not? My heart remembered ye."

Sabrina couldn't help but smile and caressed his cheek. "I'll remind you of those words when you regain your memory."

He nodded. "I hope to remember everything. Who is downstairs?"

. . .

GAVIN DIDN'T like Sabrina's evasiveness. She'd averted her eyes when he'd asked if she came to take him home. Did she not live with him?

How did he know to trust the strangers before him? True, he remembered Sabrina with fondness and the man, Tristan, was instantly familiar. Tristan's partner, Gwyneth, as well. Gwyneth was clearly Sabrina's sister and evoked trust.

After Tristan explained about an enchantment, about them living in another world, he began explaining the mechanics of leaping. "Gavin, you must will yourself back. It's imperative that you do not remain another day in this realm. You will begin aging at a fast rate, so swift you could die in a matter of weeks."

Gavin looked to Sabrina, whose hand he'd yet to release. "Will you go with me?"

Again her eyes evaded, "I can't."

"Then I refuse to go." His mind made up, he released Sabrina's hand and crossed his arms. "I wish to go home now."

A muscle in Tristan's jaw flexed. "Gavin, the alter-world is your home, for now at least. The sooner you leave, the sooner you can regain your memory and join Sabrina for good."

Sabrina spoke to Tristan. "We need to summon Liam or Padriag."

"Liam?" John spoke up, the entire time he'd remained in the background, absorbing all the interaction between Gavin and the group. "Gavin remembered the name."

"I remember the name Liam, but not any other detail about him."

When Sabrina locked gazes with him, worry lines creased her brow. "Gavin, maybe if you go back to the alter-world, you'll remember everything. The sooner you are able to remember, the faster you and I can be together."

She turned to her sister. "Let's try together. To summon Liam."

Not sure what to do, Gavin sank into a chair. Perhaps she didn't love him, didn't want him to remain with her. The alter-world sounded like a fantasy. How could he not remember any of what Tristan described?

Sabrina fought the urge to cry. The temptation to just take him back to Tristan's keep gnawed at her. Would him remaining another pair of days do more harm than good? For a split second she considered that if he didn't remember his aversion to being touched, they could make love before he left. It wouldn't be right, not in the vulnerable state he was in at that moment.

He sat down, his expression so forlorn, confused. Yet another horrible punishment from the hate-filled wizard. But she didn't have the right to make this decision for him, not right now. Unable to bear it, she sat next to him and leaned into his chest.

"The reason Meliot is throwing these hurdles at us has to be because he knows we are getting closer to breaking you knights out of the enchantment," Sabrina told him. "We need to keep going. To keep fighting."

Gavin studied the people in the room, not seeming to understand the gravity of what had happened. It was understandable.

No sooner had Sabrina concentrated on summoning Liam than he did appear, looking around with wild eyes. Then relief seemed to wash over him when he noticed Gavin. "You found him."

John looked about ready to pass out. "Another one?"

Everyone ignored him except for Liam who frowned at the pale man before turning his attention back to Sabrina.

"I will take him back, but what should we do after that?"

"Send Padriag for me," Sabrina replied. "If it's possible for me to come to the alter-world I must go. I am the only one he remembers."

"Very well." The English Knight's ice-blue eyes met hers. A flicker of something akin to distrust flashed in his gaze before he looked away. It was as if he found her lacking, for some reason. Perhaps because she was Gavin's enchantress, and the two men didn't get along.

"Hallo Gavin," Liam said. "I will take you back to our home now."

Not seeming to recognize Liam, Gavin looked to John as if for confirmation that he could trust him.

If possible, John paled further, his Adam's apple bobbed. "I am John Stewart, I found him. Outside my shop here."

"Thank you," Liam replied.

"I'm so sorry!" Sabrina exclaimed. "In all this confusion I didn't thank you John. I'm so sorry you've been dragged into all this, hopefully you don't think we're a bunch of lunatics."

John smiled. "No need. I always suspected travel between

planes was a possibility. Now I know for certain. This has been quite enlightening."

"Are ye a wizard?" Liam asked him.

"Yes, well Wiccan is what I prefer to be called." John replied. "Wiccan...er, I do try my hand at spells at times."

Gwen touched John's arm. "That's perfect. Maybe you can help us to break an enchantment that keeps them trapped in an alter-world. We may need your assistance."

John grinned, showcasing deep dimples. "Yes, of course. I would love to."

Liam grimaced. "I have to go." He looked to Gavin, who looked to her, his eyes worry-filled.

How could she let him go like this? "Can I speak to him, just for a moment please?" Sabrina took Gavin's hand and pulled him out of the room.

In the small sitting room, she met his worried gaze. "Gavin, I promise you I will help you. You will be free and come here permanently. Trust me. You and I will be together. But for now, it is imperative that you go with him."

He didn't reply, instead pressed his lips together, she could tell he debated her words.

"Look here." She took a piece of paper out of her back pocket, an image of them on it. "This was taken when we spent the day at Castle Campbell, your home in Scotland. Keep it with you. Know that I will come. I want you to stay with me too, but you can't remain in this realm. It is dangerous. You will age and die. You must go with Liam."

Finally he reached for the item, tucking it into the front pocket of sweatpants. "Very well."

"We must go." Liam stood in the room, his eyes on Gavin. "Come."

Liam wrapped his arms around Gavin who tensed, his widened eyes locking with hers.

"Close your eyes," Liam told him, his words clipped.

Then they were gone.

CHAPTER FOURTEEN

The alter-world seemed very familiar, the purplish sky, two suns shining brightly, even the hazy horizon looked familiar. The tall imposing grey stone keep with large wooden doorways and slim long arrow slits beckoned him in. Once inside, he became lost again, not sure who the men inside were, the location of his chamber a mystery, as was the reason for the large main room's light, with no torches visible.

Liam, the man who'd transported him back, spoke with barely concealed disdain. "I suppose introductions are in order." The two other men exchanged puzzled looks, but did not speak.

"This is Niall MacTavish." Liam indicated a large man with black hair whose grey eyes met his with concern. "This is Padriag Clarre, our resident wizard," Liam introduced a red-haired young man next, who grinned widely at him.

"Whoa," Padriag exclaimed, shaking his hand. "You got

amnesia? That sucks." Then he swung toward Niall. "Maybe you can fix him."

Niall nodded, but remained quiet, his somber eyes studying him. Gavin gathered the man rarely spoke. Not sure what else to do, he sat at a large table.

"Tristan explained to me the reason for our enchantment and that it is possible for us to be freed. What can you tell me about my life here?" He asked.

Again, the exchange of looks. Finally, Liam cleared his throat. "I think we should concentrate on your memory loss. Rehashing the past will do little good."

"You and Liam hate each other," Padriag told him, his eyes going between him and Liam. "Always fighting and arguing. Not sure why, but I think he's jealous because you're better looking, and he's used to being the best looking in the room."

"Shut up, Paddy," Liam snapped. "You should have been born a woman. You talk too much."

"Struck a nerve did I?" Padriag's amused look made Gavin like the young man. He must have kept them entertained through the years.

"Paddy, why don't you search in those spell books of yours for a memory spell." Niall told Padriag and then spoke to him. "I will place my hands on your head. Try to remain still."

The man's large hands cupped his head. Warmth seeped through them, calmness came with it, and Gavin closed his eyes enjoying the sensations. In his mind, pictures flashed by, sword fights, large flying beasts, followed by brightly covered beds, scenes of lovemaking, him and several women.

He didn't know how long it took before Niall removed his hands. When he opened his eyes, Niall was sitting, pale, drinking heavily from a mug.

"Healing depletes you," Gavin said. "I apologize."

Niall only shrugged. Padriag looked at him, full of expectation, his eyes bright. "Remember anything?"

"Nay, I saw many images. Battles we must have fought, flying beasts, and other things, but nothing that stood out as a memory."

"Do you remember us?" Liam asked, eyes narrowed, brow crinkled. "Do you remember me?"

Gavin studied each of their faces, finding familiarity. They were not strangers to him, but he didn't remember anything specific about them. He told them as much.

"Okay," Padriag said, "Let me try this quick spell, it's a memory spell for when someone forgets one specific thing. Maybe it will bring an important memory back."

"No," Liam said. "I do not think that is a good idea. You need to find a spell for total memory loss."

"I think he should try," Niall proposed. "What harm could come of it?"

"I agree," Gavin told them, his gaze tracking Padriag, who was walking toward him, a large book in one hand, his face serious.

Padriag stood over him and began to chant, reminding him of John's chant, a language he didn't understand. Padriag stopped chanting and gave him an annoyed look. "Close your eyes, and concentrate."

The 'quick' spell seemed to go on and on. This time Gavin did not see anything and struggled not to fall asleep.

"Fine. Open your eyes," Padriag told him impatiently. "From your yawns, I can tell it's not working."

"I'd like to go to my chamber." Gavin stood and began heading out of the room.

"Wrong way," Padriag told him, an eyebrow cocked. "You really don't remember shit do you?"

Gavin bit back the urge to curse. Why did he remember that room, but not the people here?

TORN BETWEEN RELIEF AND SADNESS, Liam watched Gavin climb the stairs behind Niall. How he hated the feelings that still tore through him each time those amber eyes landed on him, the pitch in his stomach competing against the bile in his throat over how the man once treated him.

In order to keep his word and return for Sabrina, he tried to leap back to the other realm, but couldn't. He had overextended his powers to the brink when bringing Gavin back.

Liam stared at the ceiling until Padriag nudged him. "Hey, look at this. Do you think this is a bring back memory spell, or a spell to improve memory?"

Looking at the gibberish on the page, Liam couldn't tell, so he just gave Padriag a blank stare. "I need you to go back and bring Gavin's enchantress."

"Nah, you go. I have a spell to figure out." Padriag replied.

"I've tried leaping to the other realm several times but cannot after bringing Gavin back." Liam revealed.

Padriag blew out an annoyed breath. "We don't think I

can do it. I can try, maybe later. I have to work on his memory. I think that's more important right now."

Liam bit back the urge to growl. "I promised them that I would return immediately and bring her here. She is the only person Campbell remembers."

"I get it," Padriag replied. "Well, I'm not going anywhere tonight. Unlike you, I have to go out there." He pointed toward the doorway. "I can try at sunrise and see. I'm not sure I can will myself to wherever Sabrina is."

It made sense. Centaurs and other creatures could see at night. Liam had not considered it. "Perhaps it is for the best. Gavin could possibly regain his memory after some time with Niall."

Either way, Liam would try again in the morning; it was time for him to start seeking the way to end his own enchantment. Unfortunately, he didn't see an enchantress in his future. He'd never felt a pull to return to England. Whenever he had gone to the other realm, he'd always gone to northern Scotland, a city called Carlisle, where his family had owned lands.

John Stewart was a witch, a person who could cast spells. And, Liam was certain, someone who preferred men. There had been something in the way the man had looked at him. The interest in his gaze had been more than just curiosity.

Perhaps this man was the answer to his freedom. It could be there was a glimmer of hope.

IT HAD BEEN a restless night of images whirling in Gavin's mind. So many pictures of people and places, strange beings and battles. He had awakened many times throughout the night confused and exhausted.

When the light of dawn finally came through the window, he rubbed his dry eyes and studied the surroundings. The room hadn't changed, he remained in the alterworld. In his last dream, once again, he'd been with Sabrina. Her presence had been so vivid he'd expected to wake and find her there.

Irritated and feeling groggy, he got up, dressed and went downstairs.

As he descended the stairs, the sight before him gave him pause. The great room was littered with books and papers. The young knight, Padriag, slept, his face on an open book, his soft snores the only sound except for the crackling of wood coming from the fireplace.

Not sure if he should wake him, Gavin paced the room. Its familiarity told he'd been in that room. It felt like home. But no specific memories came. Frustrated, he threw his head back and stared at the ceiling. Why couldn't he remember anything?

According to Niall, the wizard, Meliot, used all types of weapons against them. This weapon seemed formidable, insurmountable. If he could not remember, how could he be freed and help save the others?

He tapped on Padriag's shoulder. The young man bolted upright and stared up at him. "What?"

"Where is Sabrina?"

"Scotland," Padriag replied, his eyes half closed. "Liam couldn't go get her. He tried. I have to wait until sunrise." He scratched his head and yawned. "Is it sunrise?"

"I believe so," Gavin said sliding a look at the dim sky outside the window.

Chapter Fifteen

"This is probably the best thing to happen yet." Tristan's lips curved into a wide grin. "Think about it. If he cannot remember anything, he will not argue against the conditions to break his enchantment."

Astounded Sabrina couldn't stop her mouth from hanging open. Although it was true that if Gavin didn't remember his past, it would be easier to get him to make love, it felt wrong in a way. And yet, this was the answer, perhaps the only way for it to happen.

"I am not sure how I feel about it. Although he may consent to it, how will he feel once his memory returns? The act could be detrimental to his mental health."

Tristan frowned. "I do not understand what you go on about. The goal is to free him. I am sure no matter the circumstance, he will be grateful. That ye and he are intimate is not something he will regret." He seemed worried. "Liam should have returned by now."

Sabrina admired the man's attractive stance as he stalked

to the front of the room and stood by the window. Tall at over six foot three or four, his wide shoulders and muscular physique could not be diminished by his modern clothing. He preferred to wear jeans and long-sleeved pullover shirts, a far cry from the tunics and breeches more common during his time.

"Perhaps Meliot has distracted them with one of his tricks. Besides, time here and in the alter-world are very different," Sabrina suggested.

Tristan shook his head. "Have you tried to summon him? If he has regained his memory, he may need a summons. We must do something." At Tristan's obvious frustration, Sabrina wished she could do more.

"I have tried several times to no avail. We have to be patient and continue to work on what we can here. There is little we can do for them other than hope they are well enough to come when they can."

———

"YOU REMEMBER ME YET?" Padriag pointed to himself.

"You seem familiar, but I do not recall anything specific about you."

A sharp push caused him to swing around. No one stood behind him. Puzzled he drank from his cup more only to spill some when a second push caused him to bend forward.

"Oh, I think you have to go," Padriag told him, watching him closely. "Do you remember how to leap?"

"What causes this?"

"I think your enchantress is calling you," Padriag replied.

"I don't remember how to go there," Gavin said, a pang in his chest at the thought of not seeing Sabrina.

"It's not too hard. You concentrate on a location, leap there mentally and boom," Padriag told him with a shrug. "Besides, I can help you." The young knight stood and walked to a window. Peering outside while he stretched. "At least one sun is up. I'll go with you outside. We can only leap from outside the keep. Well, except for Liam. He can do it from in here."

Gavin waited for Padriag, impatient to leave. The young knight glanced toward the stairway. "I'll go tell Niall. We have a rule not to leave the keep without telling another person. Hold on." He bounded up the stairs.

The tug this time was stronger and Gavin wondered if something bad happened. Not sure what to take, he picked up a sword and scabbard. Then he grabbed an apple and slid it into a small bag, along with short dagger off the table. Padriag returned, noting he was armed, but said nothing.

Niall entered the room behind Padriag.

"Okay, let's go. Keep your eyes open. Best to unsheathe the sword. We may get one of Meliot's nasty surprises." Padriag held his sword with one hand, lifting the beam that locked the front door with the other. He opened the door slowly, peering outside. "Looks clear. Come on. I'll be right back Niall, keep an eye out for me."

They walked only a few feet from the front door. "Okay, don't hit me, I'm going to hug you." The young knight wrapped his arms around him, and they flew up. Darkness swirled faster and faster.

"Close your eyes if you don't want to throw up." Padriag

told him too late as his stomach was already threatening. He closed his eyes and coughed.

"Don't you dare throw up." Padriag told him. "I'll drop you. I don't care if you end up in Egypt."

They landed next to a creek, Padriag on his feet, Gavin on his butt in the water. "Some things never change," Padriag told him laughing. "You suck at landing."

Gavin went to get up from the shallow water, only to slip and fall back. Splashing and sputtering, he was finally able to stand and get out, Padriag's peals of laughter making the embarrassing moment even more so. When he looked up and saw Sabrina watching from a short distance, he glared at Padriag.

"Shut up, Paddy," Gavin said, repeating the words, he heard Liam use the day before. The young knight only laughed harder when Gavin bumped his head on a short branch. "Oh God, I hate that I have to go, can't wait to see what you do next." With a wide grin, he vanished.

"Goldie, you came. I was hoping you'd feel my summoning," Sabrina's smile warmed his chest. "Have you remembered anything?"

"Only I need you close to me," he replied, meaning it.

"Aw, that's so sweet," she said, taking his hand. "Come. I have something special planned for us."

He allowed her to pull him forward, enjoying the feel of her hand in his. They walked into a grouping of trees to a small secluded spot. There were several blankets and pillows on the ground, a basket beside them.

"I have a picnic planned in hopes you'd come when I summoned. We have something very important to discuss."

She sank onto the blanket, her dress falling over her long legs, the way her hair fell in waves past her shoulders.

He enjoyed the view of her for a moment before joining her.

They ate cheese, crusty bread and the apple he brought, while she told him about Tristan's enchantment and how each of them had a specific spell and condition they must meet to break free.

"I need you to listen carefully as I recount your spell and the terms of breaking the enchantment that we have discussed in the past."

At her urging, Gavin lay on his back, head on her lap, waiting for her to explain the specific terms of his enchantment. She leaned down and kissed him lightly on the lips.

SABRINA COULDN'T BELIEVE how hard it was to explain everything to him, especially the part about allowing her to make love to him. A modern woman, she'd never suffered qualms when telling a lover what she needed or wanted at a specific moment.

This time, with Gavin, she was nervous, fumbling her words. The constant thought in the back of her mind—what if he hated her when he regained his memory?

She met his amber gaze and forced herself to relax. "Alright, this is what has to happen. I will make love to you, not you to me, but me to you. You must give your body to me of your own accord without hesitation."

When Sabrina looked at him, he was looking at her with a wide grin.

"All you must do is enjoy it. That is all." Heat crept up her throat to her face. "Tell me what you are thinking."

"Whether a spell or not, I do wish to be with you. I feel excited at the prospect." He told her, his eyes already roaming her body.

"Well, there is one very important factor."

He watched her intently, listening.

"You really cannot do anything. Nothing. You cannot help me. And...you have to climax."

This time his brow furrowed as he pondered her words. "I cannot move?"

"I think you can move, I mean, of course you're going to move. Forget it. I'm going to be blunt. I will touch and kiss you all over. Take you as mine. Do you feel any hesitation in allowing it?"

His smile turned wicked with delight. Like any normal man, he didn't seem to find any problem with her plan. So far so good. Seemed he didn't remember his aversion to being touched.

"Let's get undressed."

"You first," he suggested.

She couldn't help but smile.

Men.

Standing, she unbuttoned her wraparound dress allowing it to fall at her feet. His amber eyes darkened at the sight of her black bra and thong panties. She unfastened the bra allowing it to fall next, and then she pulled her panties off and kicked them away.

"Now you."

"Am I allowed to do this myself? Isn't undressing me,

part of making love to me?" He was definitely going to use this to his advantage. She went to him and unlaced the front of his white tunic. He bent down allowing her to pull it off. His golden skin gleamed in the sunlight, muscles constricting with every move. When she kneeled to pull his boot off, he lifted one foot, then the next, the entire time his gaze glued to her.

She unlaced his breeches and pushed them down.

When his erection sprang free, she ignored the proud member and finished pulling his pants off.

Not wanting to waste time, Sabrina got to the task at hand. A quite pleasant task.

She slid her hands up his legs to hold the back of his thighs. His sharp intake of breath was music to her ears as she licked small circles on the inside of his thighs.

When her mouth took his tight sack in, his legs began trembling and she could tell he had a hard time standing. Running her tongue under the length of his erection, she kissed the tip, where a droplet of his moisture escaped. He moaned and clenched his fists.

"Lie down," She instructed him, her voice husky with want. Gavin practically collapsed on the blankets, his darkened eyes locking with her before he lay back. Moving over him, she allowed her gaze to travel his body. He was perfection.

His legs were perfectly sculpted, one bent at the knee while the other stretched out. His shallow breathing expanded his wide chest, the muscles of his flat stomach moving in unison. She placed kisses around his belly button. His hand lifted, but when she hesitated, he put it back down.

She licked and nipped him, purposely avoiding the straining member that twitched, needing her attention and kissed him deeply.

Trailing her tongue down the center of his chest, she slid her palms down his sides, loving the feel of his taut muscles.

Finally, when his hips began lifting up, she did take him fully in her mouth, her fist wrapping the base, her other hand cupping his sack. Gavin moaned loudly as he slid in and out of her mouth. He was close to release.

All thought of enchantments and curses evaporated at the heat between her legs. Her heart thundered in her chest. So far he'd not seemed to have any qualms with everything she'd done, but this was the final test. If he remembered anything, all could be lost.

Moving slowly, her eyes locked to his, she once again kissed him taking his tongue into her mouth. Breaking the kiss, her breathing ragged, Sabrina straddled him, her palms flat on his chest.

"I want you," Gavin said, gaze traveling over her body. "It is so hard not to touch you."

Her lips curved as she took his hands and placed them on her hips. Both moaned when she lowered onto his straining erection.

Little explosions of fire and passion traveled through her body as he filled her fully the thickness and length perfect. Sabrina began lifting and lowering enjoying the view as he fought not to lose control.

As she moved over him, she managed to chant the spell out loud.

. . .

By earth, by air, by fire, by sea,
I call upon the power to set thee free.
Chains unseen and binding tight,
Shatter now, by ancient light.
By flame that burns and water's flow,
The captive heart begins to grow.
No longer held by fear or might,
I summon freedom's endless flight.
By star and moon and sun above,
I break the bonds with strength and love.
The curse is dust, its hold is gone,
By will and word, the spell is done.

"Faster," he groaned out his hips lifting to meet her descents until she trembled on the brink of climaxing. When he shuddered, coming with force, she couldn't stop her own release.

Gavin began shaking, his entire body convulsing. He rolled away from her moaning, his head turning side to side. Scared, Sabrina grabbed his shoulder. "What is it?"

"I do not know." He barely was able to get the words out before he passed out.

Sabrina checked his breathing. It was normal. Placing an ear to his chest, she heard his steady heartbeat. Not sure what to do, she covered him and began to get dressed. She could try to lift him into the golf cart she'd come in and take him to the house, but he was almost over six feet tall and muscular. She doubted she could lift him on the cart. And she would not leave him here alone.

She lay beside him and wrapped her arms around him. "Gavin? Wake up sweetie. Please."

It was several moments later that his eyes opened, and he mumbled something incoherent.

Sabrina began chanting the spell again and again, smiling when a soft snore escaped his lips

Lowering herself to lay next to him, she kissed his lips and let out a sigh.

She'd let him rest for a few moments longer, then they would go to the house to see what to do next.

Something had changed and she wasn't sure if it was good or bad.

CHAPTER SIXTEEN

The sky had darkened when he gently slid away from Sabrina and got dressed. Somehow he knew without any doubt that he would not be returning to the alter-world. They had succeeded.

He was free from the curse.

Looking down at the sleeping woman, his heart expanded. He was in love with this beautiful woman. Although he could not remember much, he knew this for certain.

He crouched down and touched Sabrina's face. Did she love him? He wished he could remember any conversations they'd had prior to his memory loss.

Sabrina yawned and opened her eyes. They widened slightly, and she sprang up, sitting upright.

"Oh goodness, we have to go. Tristan and Gwen are probably wondering what we're doing." A slow smile curved her lips upward as she stood.

"You look different," she said. "You haven't grown a

beard. Oh my god! I think we did it." Her voice full of wonder, she threw her arms around his neck. "Holy crap, I can't believe it."

"Do you love me?" Why did he ask that? When her body tensed, he regretted allowing the words to escape.

She leaned back, her brow pinched. "I am not sure about that. I do care for you deeply, but it could be you doing it."

"Me doing what?" She had not said no, and he felt lighter for it.

"We'll discuss it later. Now we better head back to the house. I can't believe I fell asleep." She narrowed her eyes at him. "I can't believe you fell asleep either."

Not quite sure if he'd done something wrong, he helped her pick up the basket and blankets and load everything into the cart.

"Want to drive?"

He assisted her in climbing onto the seat, and then practically ran around to the driver's side. He wasn't quite sure how he knew it, but he knew he enjoyed driving.

"Tristan! Gwen! Come here!" Sabrina yelled after sprinting from the cart into the house. "We did it! Gavin is free!"

As he climbed from the cart, Tristan lunged forward and embraced him, and in that moment, he recalled everything about the man.

"I remember you," Gavin told him, laughing at Tristan's wide grin.

"I am glad," Tristan replied.

Gwen hugged him next, taking his face in her hands, her

lovely dark brown eyes delving into his. "I'm so happy, Gavin."

They went to a large sitting room and talked. Mostly it was Tristan telling him about their time in the alter-world.

How long they talked, he couldn't say, but it was late when Tristan and Gwen finally announced they were to retire. He looked to Sabrina, unsure.

"I had a bedroom prepared for you," Gwen told him her gaze sliding to her sister. "Unless..."

"I think it's best to let them discuss this and decide." Tristan took Gwen by the hand pulling her from the room. Gwen gave Gavin one last worried look, then allowed Tristan to take her away.

"Why is everyone hesitating about where I sleep?" Gavin asked Sabrina who studied him silently. "They know we have been intimate. Is there a social circumstance that keeps me from sharing your bed?"

Sabrina took his hand and moved closer on the couch they sat. "The reason we're worried is because it could be dangerous for me to be asleep next to you if certain memories return."

"Dangerous? I would never hurt you." Again, the fear of her leaving him came, the tightening in his chest now a familiar twinge.

"You won't hurt me. Not intentionally. But Gavin, in your past, you lived through some terrible experiences, things you do not recall. You were afraid of your reaction if you allowed a woman to make love to you. It is only because of Meliot's mistake and your loss of memory that I took the chance, otherwise we would probably have been forced to have an audience for my safety."

Hating the hurt look in her eyes, he kissed her gently, wanting to reassure her. "What happened to me?"

Sabrina hesitated not knowing if telling him about his past would bring back the nightmarish memories. He had a right to know and yet a part of her wanted to shield him from the pain that would surely come.

Finally, she relented. "Because of your attractiveness, you were kidnapped when you were a young man and sold to a sheik that preferred young men. From what I understand, you remained there for years until escaping and returning to Scotland."

His eyes widened and then narrowed. "How can I not remember it?"

Gavin got up and paced to the fireplace. Frantically he tried to remember details of what Sabrina described. She touched his arm. "Maybe you'll never remember. It would be a blessing."

Reaching for his face, she forced him to meet her eyes. "I trust you Gavin, please stay with me tonight. I need your presence, the reassurance that you're really here to stay."

LATER THAT NIGHT, listening to Sabrina's rhythmic breathing as she lay across his chest gave him some peace. He'd pretended to fall asleep after they'd made love. This time she'd allowed him to more than help her as they gave each other pleasure. The intimacy of the moment brought him to tears, his body not seeming to remember the last time he'd been able to enjoy the act of making love without fear. Now, as he looked up into the darkness, a tear slid down the side of his face. One by one the memories of his time in the Harem returned, and he grew too scared to fall asleep. Tomorrow he'd move into the other chamber. He could not risk hurting Sabrina.

THE NEXT MORNING, Gavin asked a maid to show him to his chamber. The maid, who kept staring at him and tripped twice, finally arrived at a doorway. He thanked her with smile, and she looked about to faint. He'd have to inspect his face in a looking glass. The woman's reaction didn't seem normal.

Once inside, he showered and studied his face in the mirror. A familiar set of amber eyes greeted him. His lashes seemed too long for a man. He didn't like them. His mouth was full, especially his bottom lip. There was an indentation in his chin, and his teeth were white and even. He smiled and saw two dimples appear. Those, too, he didn't like. He brushed his hair. It was a golden blonde, thick and shoulder length. Perhaps, he'd ask if he should cut it. His face, looked like a normal face. Frowning, he didn't understand the maid's reaction to his looks. Then again, his stature could be intimidating.

Someone had taken the time to purchase quite a few things for him. He suspected it was Sabrina and Gwen. Going through the clothing, he chose a pair of dark blue pants like he'd seen Tristan wear and a brown long sleeve shirt which he pulled on over his head. Satisfied after donning socks and soft brown leather shoes, he went to find Tristan.

TRISTAN LOOKED up from where he sat at a desk and, for a long moment, inspected Gavin from head to feet. "It will take me some time to become accustomed to seeing you in modern clothing. I am sure you feel the same."

"We will grow used to it." He studied the object on top of the desk where Tristan sat. "What are you doing?"

His friend grimaced and motioned to the object. "I am not sure I will ever be able to learn how to function in this modern world. Gwen is teaching me typing, the most used form of writing now. I have to form words on the screen by pushing down on these tiny objects." Tristan raked fingers through his hair leaving a disheveled mess.

Looking past him to take in the space, Gavin could understand the frustration. Just the fact that pushing a switch lightened a room was incredible.

"Something is bothering you," Tristan stated. It only made sense that after so much time together they were at the point they could practically read each other's minds.

"I remembered my time away—my time in captivity."

Tristan was silent, worry in his gaze.

"How did I deal with it? Was I ever able to function as a normal man?" Gavin asked, wishing he could remember his life after returning.

Tristan stood and walked to the window and peered out at the serene landscape. "You only spoke to me about it once. It was before the enchantment. I know that for many months you kept to yourself, barely speaking to anyone other than your brothers and parents. When you and I became acquainted, there were subtle things I noticed. You never paid mind to women. You rarely imbibed and shrank away from being touched whenever we went to the tavern."

"What else?" Gavin wanted to know everything about his past. Frustration at the long spaces of nothing grew with every moment. "Did I ever hurt anyone?"

After a moment Tristan met his gaze. "Because of your bonnie features, you were revered for it. Bards wrote songs and poems remarking on it. Women were attracted to you and at times it proved very difficult for you. After several adverse reactions on your part, it became known to stay away from you."

Gavin ground his back teeth. "You did not answer my question. Did I hurt anyone?"

"You did. Several women who were too familiar. Mostly bruising, but there was one lass whose arm you broke."

His expression must have registered shock because Tristan continued. "You were torn with guilt and made amends, paying her wages for a year so that she could recover. After that if you came to the tavern you stood at the wall and barely drank anything other than cider."

He nodded understanding and resolved to never to fall asleep when with Sabrina.

"Why does Liam dislike me so much?"

Tristan shrugged seeming to consider his words. The hesitancy wasn't a good sign. "You will have to ask him," Tristan began somewhat stilted. "Liam is a nobleman who is sometimes hard to get along with, but he is a faithful friend and ally. Sometimes I think that your constant bickering is more of a sport than actual dislike."

Gavin wasn't so sure. The tension between them was based on something. "What am I to do now?"

His friend looked at him for a long time. "Gavin, you have options, your memory is returning, once you remember more of your previous life, I have something to reveal to you."

Although he wondered what it was Tristan would show him, he was sure at the right time, he would find out.

"What about horses? Are there any here?"

Tristan's face brightened. "Aye, there are. Let us go for a ride."

GALLOPING ACROSS THE VAST ACREAGE, Gavin pushed his steed to go faster. A memory of them riding like this, fast and with determination, came so suddenly he almost lost his grip on the reins. He remembered that fateful day; the day Meliot gave them three days to prepare for their eminent departure. Into an enchantment. The memory wasn't as unpleasant as it could have been. In a way it was more bittersweet. To remember something so important and life changing was a good thing.

The cool wind, the muscular steed and the lush green countryside alleviated the tension of constantly trying to remember so many things. Concentrating on the moment and nothing else, for the first time since losing his memory Gavin felt at ease. Whatever the future brought would come weather he remembered things or not.

. . .

"Well, there you are," Gwen greeted them as they made their way into the house later that day. Tristan kissed her, hugging her to him.

"Did you even practice your typing today?" Gwen admonished, not able to keep her stern look when Tristan gave her an innocent smile.

"Gavin needed to get out." Tristan's eyes flashed to Gavin.

"Aye, I needed to go out," Gavin stammered seeing Gwen's narrowed eyes. "I remember more," he finished.

"Really?" Gwen's expression changed to excitement, her eyes rounding. That is when he noticed Sabrina, pacing in the adjoining room. With a device to her ear, she spoke in rapid tones, a hand waving in the air. It seemed the conversation was not a pleasant one.

Gavin pulled his gaze away from Sabrina when a maid appeared and announced dinner was to be served shortly.

Instead of coming with them to the dining room, Sabrina went to the library with the device still to her ear and closed the door.

As they sat down to eat, she dropped into the chair next to him and leaned over to kiss him on the cheek. "You looked handsome with your wind-tousled hair," she whispered into his ear.

Although her comment set his mind at ease, it was

obvious something bothered her as she barely spoke during the meal.

Gwen glanced at him with a silent question, and he shrugged. He was sure whatever bothered Sabrina had nothing to do with him.

"Is something wrong, Sabrina?" Gwen asked. "You seem bothered. Was it the conversation earlier?"

"I'm sorry," Sabrina replied, putting her fork down. "Mostly work issues, but then Tammie made me angry. Said she'll probably not come to Scotland."

"Why?" Gwen asked and then added. "You should've let me talk with her. What reason did she give you?"

"She said Mom told her not to come. That her future will be impacted forever and that there were dangerous hurdles in her path. Mom pretty much forbid it."

Gavin considered their conversation. In truth, being that both Gwen and Sabrina had traveled to the alter-world where many kinds of dangers could befall them, their mother's prediction was not invalid.

"I'll call Mom after dinner." Gwen told them. "I am sure she's being over-protective of Tammie. She only knows portions of what we've done here so far, but I am sure she has picked up on more than we say when we speak to her."

Tristan cleared his throat, "I am hopeful you can clear things up and we can move forward. We still have three men to free."

Gwen placed her hand over his. "We'll find a way to free them all."

Sabrina's eyes met Gavin's, then moved to his mouth. Slowly her lips curved into a wickedly sensuous smile.

It had the desired effect, his body immediately reacting.

He opened his mouth to say something, but no words came to mind. What to say to someone who enveloped every bit of his thoughts? There was no denying that he'd fallen in love. Not something born of gratitude or of desire. When he looked at her and held her at night, all he could think was that he never wanted to spend a day without her.

Taking a drink from his glass of water, he could barely swallow past the constriction the emotion had caused in his throat.

"Are you alright?" Sabrina asked, covering his hand with hers. "You look a bit odd."

"I remembered some things today," Gavin said attempting to move her attention away from his countenance. "I remember the days leading up to the enchantment."

"That is amazing," Sabrina cried out kissing his cheek. "I am so happy."

Gwen's expression was warm when she looked to him. "I am sure you will regain all of the rest."

"I have something important to discuss with Gavin, in private," Tristan told them pushing away from the table.

It was hard to tell by Tristan's neutral expression what he wished to discuss. Gavin didn't question his friend. He'd find out soon enough.

Gwen stood. "I think its best that I call Mom. It is still quite early in the day in Georgia."

"I want to listen in." When Sabrina pushed away from the table, Gavin stood and pulled back her chair. At the press of her lips to his, Gavin's heart fluttered. At this rate, he'd be seeing butterflies circling every time she paid him any attention.

The sisters walked from the dining room, discussing how to best approach the conversation with their mother. Gavin got the impression Iona Lockhart was a force to be reckoned with.

Gavin followed Tristan just past the kitchen to a locked door. Tristan unlocked the door, flipped a light switch and proceeded down a dimly lit wooden staircase.

They entered a large wine cellar that smelled of wine, oak and what could only be described as the scent that came from years of undisturbed surroundings. On a table, there was a candle tipped to one side next to matches.

Tristan indicated a wine rack. "Help me move this," he instructed and together they pushed it sideways. Other than cobwebs, the stone wall resembled the others enclosing the room.

After studying the stones, Tristan pressed on one with the heel of his hand until there was a creaking sound revealing a jagged doorway.

"Did you make that?" Gavin asked moving closer to inspect the handiwork.

"No," Tristan replied. "Perhaps my grandfather. It is but a wooden door with a stone façade." He motioned to Gavin. "Come."

Tristan held up what looked to be a torch by the light emanating from it.

"The modern torch is much better than our flaming ones, you do not think?" Tristan asked with a grin holding the item up.

Past the doorway there were stone steps in a dim tunnel. They descended the stairs until ending up in a large cave. Fresh air flowed through, revealing that this had to be an escape route for the family in case of attack.

They turned into the cave until reaching a small enclave where several dark wooden boxes were tucked into the crevices.

The light from the torch illuminated a naturally formed shelf on which five coffers sat.

Tristan cleared his throat. "Prior to leaving, I packed these coffers. One for each of us, so that when we returned, we would have coin in case our family and fortunes did not survive. I was the most fortunate they were never discovered. I suspect no one else in our group has such."

Gavin stared at his friend, not quite sure what to say. The fidelity of the man who stood before him was incredible. "I cannot accept ...."

"The hell you will not!" Tristan interrupted. "Everything was all my fault. It was I who convinced you to join me on that cursed trip."

Gavin stepped forward; he saw the coffer with each of their names on it. Behind his, another smaller one. "Why do I have two?"

Tristan pressed his lips together, his eyes meeting Gavin's. "Look at the seal and see if you recognize it."

Gavin took the flashlight and moved closer, he pushed the larger heavy coffer aside. The seal on the smaller coffer was the Campbell coat of arms. His brother's seal. Legs giving out, he stumbled back. His brother had come and left something for him.

"I will wait for you at the cave's exit. Take three lefts and then two rights, follow the scent of fresh air."

ONCE TRISTAN WALKED AWAY, Gavin took the small box. With trembling hands, he lowered the coffer to the ground. It weighed heavy.

The pounding in his chest echoed in his ears as he lifted the top. The coffer was filled with gold coins, atop them, a rolled parchment.

Falling back to sit, he leaned on the cool cave wall, holding the parchment. For a long time he just held it. Emotions threatened to overcome hm as he considered that his brother had held this very item in his hands. His family, long gone, had possessed the gold and coffer.

Reverently, Gavin unrolled the parchment and read the still familiar swirls of his brother's handwriting.

BROTHER MINE,

I trust if ye read this, it means ye are finally free.
It has been thirty years since ye left.
Our mother, torn with grief, insisted that we hold a
burial and place a stone marker with yer name in
the family graveyard. Understand, it was her way
of dealing with losing her eldest son. Ten years after
ye were gone, she died peacefully in her sleep.
Our uncle's leadership as Laird is lacking and our clan
is divided. We warred with the McLeods. Many of yer
men died because of it.

Now finally we have separated from The Campbell's of
Argyll and, joined with the Campbells of Devonshire.
We live in peace.
I am almost sixty years of age and wished to make
this trek to leave ye something before my health
would nae longer allow it.
Know that I am proud of ye and live in hope of
yer return.
Thomas Campbell

GAVIN GAVE WAY TO GRIEF; sadness for what his clan suffered because of his departure. Sobs racked through him, his entire body shuddering. Never before had he felt so much sorrow or loss. He grieved for the lost years, for the stolen moments of his youth, his family and the promise of what his life could have been.

Unsure how much time had passed, he turned once again to the coffer to return the parchment. To him it was worth much more than the gold.

It could have been minutes or an hour before he stood with the small coffer under his arm and went to find Tristan.

His friend stood at the cave entrance, keeping silent watch. The sun had fallen, giving the surroundings a purplish hue. For a moment it reminded him of the alterworld's sky.

Tristan didn't turn to him when he approached.

"There was a letter from my brother, Thomas. He brought the coffer many years after we were gone."

Tristan nodded. "My brother must have placed it there

with the others." He met Gavin's gaze. "Your brother was a great man."

A vision of the tall broad-shouldered Thomas, almost his same height, golden hair and stern expression formed. He'd caught glimpses of the family when he'd willed himself to his childhood home. But many years passed between the visits each time he did, it was painful to note the passage of time.

"The gold is worth a great deal. Ye will not need for anything. Gwen tells me each of you can afford homes and anything required for a comfortable life," Tristan explained.

Gavin nodded. "I don't expect to leave here until the others are free. If that is acceptable to you, of course."

"I agree that we should all remain as close as possible." Tristan motioned to where several large structures remained. They looked like large cottages. "You can afford to live anywhere in the world, but I hope you stay here. The homes are quite large. Edith, the latest descended of mine who ran the estate, assured me they were always well maintained."

"I will accept your offer," Gavin told his friend, extending his hand. "I insist on work to earn my keep."

Tristan smiled, shaking his hand. "I was hoping you'd ask. I need someone to take over the horse breeding portion of the estate. You have always been great with beasts. They don't seem to care if you're the fairest of them all and are not distracted by your pretty face."

Gavin punched his shoulder lightly. "Shut up McRainey."

Chapter Seventeen

After speaking to their mother, Sabrina and Gwen gave up. It was best to speak to Tammie and allow her to decide.

Sabrina wondered if, instead, they should heed their mother's warning. "If Mom isn't comfortable with our sister coming, perhaps we need to reconsider asking Tammie to come."

Gwen sat back, shaking her head. "I suppose if Tammie doesn't feel any kind of nudge to come, then she may not be part of this."

Sabrina glanced toward the doorway. Gavin and Tristan had not returned from wherever they'd gone. Almost three hours had passed since they'd left.

"What could they possibly be discussing?" she asked.

"I think Tristan is filling him in on their financial situation." Gwen replied.

"Imagine coming back to this realm after centuries. Not

only will it take time to get used to everything, but they don't have anything. No identification, no way to make a living. My heart breaks for them."

Gwen waved a hand in the air as if it were inconsequential. "They have willed themselves here over the years, so they have an idea of the changes. Not just that, but our trips to Edinburgh have been to meet with people who will help with such things as identification and such. Since they will not be living complicated lives, they should be okay for a bit."

"How will they make a living? They still need money," Sabrina asked wondering how her sister was taking the issue so lightly.

"They all have plenty of money," Gwen replied, smiling when Sabrina's eyes widened. "Tristan said Gavin has even more, his brother, the laird, left a coffer of gold here for him."

"What about the others?"

This time Gwen stood and stretched. "Tristan hid a coffer for each of them before leaving. Each one is filled with gold that is worth millions now. They won't ever have to worry about an income."

"It may be complicated to claim it." Sabrina considered that the authorities would wonder about coffers found.

"Edith is meeting with lawyers to figure out the best way to do it. The coffers will stay where they are, the location not divulged until it can be done without any chance of losing them." Gwen took in her expression. "Stop worrying. The lawyer told us that since it is found on McRainey land, every bit of it will be considered Edith's property. Once the gold is sold, then accounts will be set up for each man.

"Where are the coffers now?"

"There is an area below this house that is accessible by caves. Tristan likes to go there. It reminds him of the past," Gwen told her, with a faraway look on her face. "I know it will be an adjustment for them. There are times when Tristan is restless with worry about the others."

Sabrina went to her sister and placed a hand over hers. "He has you, Gwen, and now Gavin."

"He pushes himself too hard. Sometimes I wake at night to find him pacing or standing by a window. He can't seem to rest."

The amount of trauma the damn wizard caused would linger for many years. Each of the men would be facing demons of their own in finding their freedom. And then there was the new life, which would bring a new set of situations.

Sabrina studied her sister. "We need to look at the good parts of this. Like the fact that you are married to a rich hottie and living in this amazing place."

"What about you?" Gwen asked.

"I'm leaving, of course. I can't stay here forever. But for now, I'm sleeping with a hunk." She kept her voice light, ignored the stirring in her chest. "I have a photo shoot coming up. The Japanese company finally approved the models. But hey, the Marc Jacobs photo shoot in a couple of months will be here, in Scotland, so I will be back then."

Gwen frowned. "What the hell are you talking about Sabrina? What about Gavin? You can't just walk out on him."

"What do you want me to do?" Sabrina ran both hands down her face. "Be with a man who can't be touched? To live in fear that while making love he will snap my neck or something? No matter how much I love someone, how could I deal with that? Besides, I have to get back to my life."

Before her sister could say anything, she continued. "Not all of us are meant to have your fairy tale ending Gwen. You get to keep the prince. I only got to kiss one."

"Fine. Go ahead, do what you want. But at least give him a few days to adjust to being here before you break his heart," Gwen snapped, then stormed from the room.

"What am I supposed to do?" Sabrina called after her.

SABRINA WENT to her bedroom not waiting for Gavin's return. To her surprise she woke up the following morning still alone in the bed. He'd not come to join her.

A soft knock sounded, and she called whoever it was to enter. Hannah, one of the maids, entered with tea. "Your sister sends this."

Since they were young, Gwen would always send her tea if they had any kind of disagreement. It was comforting that some things never changed.

"Thank you," Sabrina replied. "Are Laird McRainey and the Mr. Campbell awake yet?"

Hannah smiled brightly, her cheeks coloring at the mention of the men. "Oh yes, miss, they've left for the stables, had a very early breakfast."

Sabrina took the sip of tea. Gavin was avoiding her.

If she was to leave and return to work, there was much

work to do before she could leave. Whenever Gavin was prepared to speak to her, he'd do so. Sabrina dressed in a pair of jeans and an oversized Georgia University sweatshirt and went downstairs to the library.

Gavin wasn't present at the noon meal either. Tristan told her he'd decided to take his meal with Miles at the stable.

"Let's be honest, he is avoiding me. Is it because of the fact he can't be intimate with me? Or something else?"

Tristan shrugged. "I am not privy to what he is thinking. It could be he needs time to consider things."

"We don't have the luxury of time. There are important things to work on, like the other men who are trapped."

Sabrina pushed back from the table and stalked out of the room and the front door. Once outside, she hurried to one of the golf carts and headed in the direction of the stables.

Once there, she walked through and peered into the stalls. Besides a mare with a bandaged leg, the rest were all empty.

"Is anyone here?" Sabrina called out and Miles appeared holding a broom. "What can I do for you, miss?"

When she asked about Gavin's whereabouts, Miles instructed her to go around the back through the large opening.

There were two large fenced in areas. In one corral horses grazed, their long tails swishing back and forth. In the other, a horse galloped around the perimeter with Gavin atop it.

She wasn't sure if he saw her, but Gavin jumped from the horse when it barely slowed and slapped it on the rump allowing the animal to continue on.

Hair wind-tossed and cheeks pinkened from the air, he looked very much like a medieval highlander. His expression was hard to read as he walked with long strides toward her.

"Has something happened?" His amber eyes searched her face.

Sabrina wanted to snap, but she kept her voice neutral. "Nothing new. I didn't see you last night. Everything ok between us?"

"Tristan and I returned late. I did not wish to disturb you. Came out here early to become familiar with the horses and see how things are done. I work here now, training the horses and handling the breeding program." His voice so filled with pride, she almost forgave him for avoiding her.

"That's awesome."

"What is this word 'awesome?'" he asked.

"It means great, good."

He smiled again, his deep dimples melting her knees. Could she handle it? The man was so gorgeous it was almost scary.

"You didn't come to bed last night."

He tensed but then shrugged as if nothing was wrong. "Everything is verra well. It was late," he repeated.

Deciding not to dwell on the subject for now, she looked up at him. "We need to talk."

He shook his head. "Aye we can, but later. I do not have time now. I have to prepare for people who will arrive soon to discuss breeding. Tristan and Miles want me present. That is what I was going to come and tell you, that I will come to you later, after they take their leave."

Sabrina shook her head. "You have to learn to speak differently, say 'yes' and 'no' for starters all right?"

"Yes." He leaned forward and kissed her.

Seeing Tristan approach, he gave her a second quick peck on the lips and walked away.

"Well, I guess I have to wait for my man to come home after work," Sabrina mumbled, heading back to the golf cart.

CHAPTER EIGHTEEN

L iam joined the other two men at the midday meal. The air was thick around them, each man with different emotional reactions to Gavin's absence.

"He's free," Padraig said, his chin resting on his hands, his dinner untouched in front of him. "And then there are three."

"Aye," Niall said, not seeming to be bothered as he bit into a chunk of meat.

"I wonder if the third sister has arrived?" Liam asked.

He'd barely slept, unable to figure out how he felt about Gavin's absence. A part of him was relieved that he'd not have to see the man daily and be reminded of a moment in his life he wished to forget. Another made him anxious that more changes were on the horizon.

"I'll go and see," Padraig said, brightening. "I know that wench is meant for me."

"Nay," Niall told them, his solemn grey eyes meeting Liam's. "Stewart will go."

Padraig actually pouted. "Why him? I should go."

"Liam can leap from inside the keep. I am worried that with two being free, Meliot may know and bring more danger."

Liam nodded. "It's even more dangerous now that it's darkening season," he said, referring to the time when only the smaller of the suns shone, giving the days a dim light that resembled just before sun fully set in the other realm. A twilight sort of haze.

Despite his silence, Niall was their cornerstone, a solid force that gave the men a sense of strength. Liam looked to him. "I have not been able to see the near future. Something has been in the way."

"It could be because it is your own destiny that awaits," Niall replied.

Liam had thought the same. For some reason, his ability had always been limited when it came to himself. "Right, I best go so we can be reassured that Gavin is indeed free now.

A pang of something akin to sadness overtook him when he looked to the two men who peered at him with expectation. He didn't want to leave them behind.

IT WAS a sunny day in the other realm, the warm breeze greeting him with the fragrance of fragrant lilies.

Gavin and Tristan stood next to a corral talking, next to them an item he recognized as a form of transportation called a golf cart.

Tristan reacted first, lifting his hand in acknowledgement,

walking toward him. Gavin's reaction was more reserved, the Scot only looking at him, his expression more wary. Even if he didn't remember him, he sensed they were not friends.

"Liam, you've come to check on Gavin?" Tristan said by way of greeting and then lowered his voice, "his memory is returning, but he still does not remember many things."

"He has been released from the enchantment then?" Liam asked, noticing that Gavin had yet to join them.

"Aye." Tristan gave him a worried look.

"The third sister is resistant to traveling here. Both Gwen and Sabrina are working to convince her. But we have also begun searching for other enchantresses. Come, let us go to the house."

He joined them in the cart contraption. The drive to the large home was quick. Gavin drove fast, making Liam nervous. It was not only the speed that caused his consternation. It was not understanding how the cart was able to move without being pulled.

Tristan laughed when they came to a stop and Liam was slow to release the bar he'd gripped until his knuckles had turned white.

Without a word, Gavin went straight inside and up the stairs.

"I think you should talk to him," Tristan told Liam.

"I do not think he wishes to speak with me," Liam replied, a knot forming in his gut.

"It is your choice, of course," Tristan said as they entered. Immediately his expression brightened at seeing Gwen in the sitting room.

"Liam, I'm so glad you're here," Gwen exclaimed waving him over. "Sabrina and I are planning a gathering."

He and Tristan exchanged questioning looks.

"Yes, a magical gathering." Sabrina clarified. "We will invite people who are strong in magic."

Gwen spoke next. "It will be in a pair of days. The three of you should remain on alert, hopefully one or all will feel the pull and know their enchantress is here."

"We decided having a group could move things along at a faster pace," Sabrina said.

"Grand idea." Tristan kissed Gwen's temple making Liam's heart lighten at the sight. Through all the years, he'd not ever considered seeing any of the men with partners. It felt good to see it.

"Where's Gavin?" Sabrina asked.

"I believe he went to bathe," Tristan said, moving to a side bar to pour drinks. "How are things in the alter-world, Liam?"

"All is well. Quiet for now. I came to ensure Gavin was indeed free and not lost again." Liam spoke for a few moments longer, telling them of the thoughts of the other men, how they worried that Meliot would make things harder if he sensed Gavin had escaped.

For a while, they discussed what could be done and still Gavin didn't return.

Liam glanced to the stairwell. "I will speak to Gavin, then I must leave."

"Third room on the left," Gwen informed him.

Despite the lack of memory, Gavin sensed tension between them, and it was best to give him clarity. Liam wasn't exactly sure what he'd say, but the words would come.

The corridor was well lit, large glass paned windows flanking the entire outside wall. Liam's leather boots sank into the plush carpeting as he headed to where Gavin was. The closer he got, the harder his heart pounded. Arriving at the slightly ajar door, he knocked.

Gavin sat on the bed, his hair wet, pulling on shoes. The immediate tightness of his jaw told he did indeed remember Liam.

"What do you want Stewart?" Gavin asked, meeting his gaze.

"So you remember me. I suppose this means you are glad not to be living in the same place."

Gavin didn't respond right away. He closed his eyes for a moment, then stood, towering over him. "I am not glad to be away from the three of you. I will work along with the others and not rest until you are free."

"We should talk." Liam began.

"You should go," Gavin said. "I am sure the sisters have questions that can help with the spell to free you."

"Listen to me." Liam waited for Gavin to meet his gaze. "Despite that we've never gotten along, I am very glad that you are free." He closed the distance. "I am man enough to admit that I do miss your presence."

He knew he should stop, but he couldn't hold back the resentment he'd managed to keep a hold on for so many years.

"The truth is that I loved you, Gavin, loved you for many years. I hated the fact that I did, but I'm man enough to admit it. I know you are glad to be rid of me. Glad to forget me."

Gavin stood and neared. Liam held his breath. If the man was going to strike him, he'd take it and not fight back. He was too tired to fight back.

Instead Gavin took him by the shoulders. "I love you as well, Liam."

Liam gawked at him. "Wh-what?"

"Like I love Tristan, Niall and Padriag. How could I not? We have all lived through years of hell, years of torment together. To forget you; it would be like forgetting a brother. I apologize again for the way I treated you. I cannot go back and change my actions. Please accept my offer of friendship."

Gavin took a step back and held his hand out.

Liam stared at his hand, the hand of the man he'd always love like a brother. Slowly he reached forward, Gavin closed the distance closing his larger hand over his. "Friends?"

He could only nod. Then he willed himself away, not wanting Gavin to see the tears that spilled.

Thankful that the men were obviously already in bed when he arrived back at the keep, Liam went straight to his room.

Years of resentment, of not knowing how Gavin felt, of fearing he'd lost a friend, fell away as he lay in bed and cried.

Outside lightening crossed the sky, the brightness flashing into the room and he looked toward the window.

Meliot knew another knight was free.

Things were about to get worse.

Chapter Nineteen

"*I love you as well, Liam.*"

Sabrina stumbled away from the door and down the hallway the moment she heard the words, covering her mouth with both hands. So that was the reason Gavin couldn't make love with a woman?

He preferred men.

Sabrina ran into her room and closed the door, blindly stumbling toward the bed. Gavin and Liam?

"*I love you as well Liam.*"

He'd admitted to loving the man.

The door opened and she didn't need to look to know who'd entered. The mattress sank down when he sat next to her, and she allowed him to wrap an arm around her.

"You overheard part of our conversation, did you not?"

She nodded. "Yes, I did." She faced him, hating the tears in her eyes. "You don't have to explain anything. If you want to be with Liam, we'll find a way to free him."

"I do not love Liam that way."

"I heard you Gavin. You told him you loved him. It's fine. I totally get it. You can't help who you love."

With his right hand cupped under her chin, Gavin lifted her face. "Aye, you heard me tell Liam I loved him, but you must have left before hearing the rest of what I said."

Sabrina waited to hear the rest.

"I told him that I love him as a brother, just as I love Niall, Tristan and Padriag."

"Are you sure? Because if you are gay...prefer men, then it would be fine. It's fully accepted nowadays for people of the same sex to be together."

Gavin shook his head. "I prefer women. I do not find men attractive, not in a sexual manner."

Although somewhat relieved, she still sensed the wall he'd erected between them. "Then why do I feel as if you're pulling away from me, Gavin?"

He pressed a soft kiss on her lips. "Because I have to keep away from you." He pressed a finger over her lips, stopping her from saying anything. "I remembered my time away, kept in a harem. I do not trust that I can be with you and not hurt you."

Keeping her emotions in check, she could only nod. "Do you want to talk about it?"

"Not now." He didn't seem upset, just quiet. Sabrina didn't know him well enough to figure out where his thoughts were.

"I'm going to stay until the gathering," Sabrina said. "Then I have to return to America. I have work commitments." She noticed Gavin tensing, but no other reaction. "I will be back in a couple of months. I have some work here in Scotland. I will come and see you then."

Gavin only nodded and stood. "I see." He looked down at her, his lips in a firm straight line. "I am not sure what I can offer you right now Sabrina. I can't be intimate with you. Not right now. My priority has to be the freedom of the three who remain. I cannot ask you to remain. It would not be fair to you."

"I understand. Believe me when I say, I do not feel any anger or resentment for anything. They are the priority. They are what keeps me here for now."

It was true, she wanted more from him but would never demand it. The poor guy still had so much to deal with. Like Tristan, his focus would be on helping the other three gain their freedom. Their relationship could not be more important than that.

The fact that her heart broke was her issue and a problem she would not burden him with.

"I'm glad you're free Gavin. You deserve a bountiful life. I am confident the others will be free soon. With Tristan and Gwen's support, not to mention the rest of the McRainey's, you have a great future in store." She smiled bravely at him.

"I will see you in the morning." Gavin kissed her, his mouth covering hers, the touch filling her with need for him. She wrapped her arms around his neck and kissed him back allowing the feel of him to fill her.

When he pulled away, his eyes had darkened. A smile curved his lips. "Until morning."

Sabrina went straight to the bed and fell back on it.

The thought of not being with Gavin hurt, and she prayed that they would be able to work through things.

Chapter Twenty

The McRainey estates buzzed with an unusual energy as people from far and wide came for the grand gathering of people with arcane talents. Hoping for progress in breaking the curses, or even for one of the men to feel a pull to someone, Sabrina and Gwen had poured themselves into every meticulous detail, working tirelessly for days, preparing for what lay ahead.

Gavin and Tristan dove into the very memories that haunted them and had thrown themselves into every conversation, piecing together their first encounter with Meliot and the meetings with the arcane beings they'd sought out—the witches, warlocks, and enchantresses whose magic held both hope and mystery.

Despite the sleepless nights and fraying nerves, a fierce determination gripped everyone in the house. They were fatigued but unyielding and had steeled themselves to face whatever challenge lay ahead. They would do whatever it took to free the three men still bound in the alter-world.

. . .

As GAVIN and Tristan approached the main house, the faint hum of voices and laughter began to fade, signaling the end of the gathering. From the shadows, they watched as guests trickled away.

The last few guests called out their goodbyes, voices laced with camaraderie of what they had in common.

"I hope they discovered something useful or that Naill or Padriag felt a something," Gavin mused as they watched from a safe distance.

Tristan nodded.

Gavin noted that Sabrina remained at the area where they'd gathered, speaking to a petite blonde. She nodded at something the woman said, then threw her head back and laughed.

He'd not seen her so relaxed and unguarded in a long time. With the perfect setting of the gentle breeze shifting her hair away from her face, she was a welcome sight. They all deserved a respite from all that occurred. Unfortunately, any opportunity was scant with the challenges they faced.

SUDDENLY LIAM APPEARED and both he and Tristan looked to him with expectation.

"Were you the lucky one that felt the pull to come?" Tristan asked.

The Englishman gave a one-shouldered shrug. "I did not, but I do find it easier than usual to will myself here and back."

"What of the others?" Gavin asked impatiently.

"They did not feel a pull either, as far as we could tell. Padriag perhaps, but we think he is just eager."

If Padriag was freed before Niall and Liam, it would be very dangerous as they'd no longer have his wards in place to keep them safe.

Gavin started to ask about Niall but didn't. If Niall had felt any sort of urgency, Liam would have told them. Instead he motioned toward the house.

"All of those gathered today met here on the estate, then they split into three groups. Each one concentrating on a different man by turn to make it easier to distinguish which person compelled whom."

They began walking toward the house and Gavin hung back to speak softly to Liam. "Have you considered speaking to John again?"

Liam shook his head. "I am not sure about him being the one who will save me, although he is persistent in helping. Of course I am willing to try." Liam didn't meet Gavin's gaze.

"You must try."

Liam nodded.

Their friend must have overheard because Tristan turned and met Liam's gaze. "John is here. I agree with Gavin in that you should spend more time with him."

When they arrived at the house, John appeared, as if summoned. He stopped short at the door and moved back so that they could enter.

When his regard landed on Liam, his cheeks pinkened. "I was about to come and get you. The gathering just ended."

"We saw," Gavin said. "We were discussing that it may be possible that you are the one who will break Liam's curse."

Once again the younger man lifted his gaze to Liam and visibly swallowed. "I—er...I did write down the beginnings of a spell ..."

"Unfortunately, I cannot leave the alter-world yet," Liam interrupted. "I am the only one who can leave from inside the keep. It has become more and more dangerous. We are surrounded constantly, unable to go outside without the possibility of being speared through."

Both Gavin and Tristan were speechless at Liam's selflessness. Gavin spoke first. "Things are bad then?"

Liam nodded. "Aye, Meliot's horsemen are back. Not only that, but the wizard must have sensed your departure, because the surroundings have totally changed, the woods are gone now; the entire area around the keep is barren, like a desert. We don't know how far it goes."

Gavin's heart sank.

"Padriag has tried without success to summon the royals of Atlandia. He makes a sport of throwing fireballs at the horsemen, as they have no place to hide. Today he only stopped because a centaur shot an arrow at him, barely missing the side of his head."

"Can you possibly help them leap here?" Tristan asked. "That will allow for each to be able to come if they feel the pull to an enchantress."

"I tried with Paddy, but it did not work. When I leaped with Gwen I was able to, so I am not sure if it's because he's enchanted, or because of Meliot's wards."

"We will have to find out if we can help them be able to

travel from inside the keep with the help of those who possess magic," Tristan said.

As if on cue, Sabrina and Gwen came through the doorway. When they spotted the men, they stopped talking. Both ran to Liam hugging him tightly and kissing his cheeks.

"Oh good, you are here. Does this mean you are the next one to be free? Did you feel the pull?" The women spoke over each other excitedly.

"I am not sure," Liam replied, his face softening at the women's attentions. Gavin understood. Missing the touch of other humans was one of the things they spoke of often during the many years in captivity. Although lucky to have each other, it was not the same as being hugged and kissed by loved ones.

After giving another few hugs to Liam, the women went to John next and began talking about the formulation of the perfect spell. All of the men in the room exchanged questioning looks as it seemed the women assumed it was John who would free Liam.

"Tell the others how hard we are trying," Gavin told Liam. "As you can see everyone is doing what they can to help free the three of you."

Tristan gave Liam a searching look. "I understand your reluctance to leave before the others, but we have to consider that if there is an order to things, we must follow it."

LIAM CONSIDERED for a long moment how strange it was that perhaps the handsome man, John, was who he was meant to be with. Each time he was in the same room with John, a longing took over that he did his best to ignore.

If he wasn't meant to be freed, he wasn't sure he'd be able to withstand the heartache that allowing himself to grow close to John would bring.

In truth, there was a possibility it was already too late. The effort it took to drag his gaze away from John proved how strong the bond between them could grow.

As John spoke with the women, his head bent over notes, Liam took the opportunity to study his profile. He was attractive, in a scholarly fashion, with disheveled wavy dark hair, soft greyish eyes and dark slants for eyebrows.

A bit shorter than Liam, John was of slender build, perfect for the protector in Liam to hold.

Just then, he realized Gavin was speaking and then turned to listen. "...I do not know if we are to truly be forever with the person who breaks our spells, but we will owe them a lifetime of gratitude."

Sabrina looked over at Gavin, taking him in with an expression of uncertainty considering the furrow that formed between her brows.

"What is happening between you two?" Liam finally asked, having seen the exchange. "Is something wrong?"

"Nothing is wrong Liam," Gavin told him, moving to pour another drink. "Tell me, are you sure Niall did not feel anything? I worry about him. He has stated on several occasions that he does not wish to leave the alter-world, but instead prefers to remain and perish at the end of the enchantment. To join his family."

Apparently, speaking about Sabrina was off limits.

"I wonder the same. If he sensed anything, he hid it well," Liam replied.

"Tell Paddy we will find who his enchantress is. You should speak with John and make plans for yourself before you have to return."

"Can we talk?" Liam asked approaching John. The man nodded and together they walked from the room and into the library.

Once they entered, John placed the notebook he carried on a table and looked up at him.

He was attracted to John, there was no denying it. Everything about the man made him want to hold him close, to kiss him. Liam cleared his throat and looked to the book.

"You said you had part of a spell written?"

Just the thought of being freed made him want to spirit himself away, back to the alter-world. Better the devil one knew and all of that.

Seeming to sense Liam's sudden thoughts of wishing to leave, John took his hand and led him to sit. "Tell me, what are you thinking? I want to help you, but I sense reluctance on your part." The man's gaze met his.

"I am needed there. I do not want to lose the opportunity to be freed, but at the same time, how can I come here and leave them behind?"

John's lips curved into a soft smile. "I was told that above all, you are honorable and loyal."

Squeezing John's hand, Liam wished it was more than just a touch. The war within him raged and he had to pull his hand away. "I am not sure about anything. How I feel. What should I do? I never dared to dream the opportunity would come for me to be freed, and now I find I am unprepared."

"This may be the one time you will have to put yourself first. This may be part of your curse, to break your own rules of honor." John searched his face. "The obstacles of your curse are that you allow yourself freedom to be your true self. What is the other half?"

"A betrayal," Liam said past a knot forming in his throat.

Liam couldn't pull his eyes away, he was definitely deeply attracted to John. He couldn't deny it. "I must go soon. Can I ask that you remain here in this house? I understand it is a great deal to ask."

Straightening his glasses, John pondered. "I suppose I can ask Tristan if it's all right."

"Tristan will agree with you staying." Seeing the look of uncertainty cross John's features, he felt selfish for asking John to bring his life to a standstill for him. "I am sorry John. I have not taken into consideration that perhaps you are not emotionally free." His stomach pitched waiting for John's reply.

"There is no one. I do have the bookstore; it's my livelihood, well besides my book sales. I am a writer and have actually made a name for myself. I write fantasy romance." With a chuckle he shook his head. "I am so writing this story."

Liam wasn't sure what the man went on about. When they had more time, he would get to know everything about John. At the moment, there were more pressing matters.

"I don't know what I can offer you in exchange for your willingness to wait for me, perhaps to give us an opportunity to get to know each other." Liam said annoyed at the hopeful tone of his voice.

John took his hand again, this time sending a jolt of passion, attraction and desire through Liam. The sensations were so strong, his body seemed to hum. For the first time in his long life it was as if his soul reacted to finding its mate. How was this possible? He'd longed for Gavin for so many years and not once had his entire being reacted so strongly.

Without thought, Liam leaned toward John and cupped his face. "Can I kiss you?"

John nodded, his eyes locking to his for a moment before moving to Liam's lips.

When he took John's mouth with his, Liam almost cried at the awareness of being with who he was meant to be with. He pushed harder, his tongue deep in John's mouth, tasting, probing, taking.

For his part, John raked his fingers through Liam's hair pressing closer, responding to the kiss with soft moans.

They broke the kiss and pressed their foreheads together, neither willing to move away first.

The tug to return to the alter-world was hard to ignore, but just as difficult was the need to stay with John for a moment longer.

"I will work on the spell," John said in a hoarse whisper. "I am certain to finish it soon, then we can try it. If I am not the one who is to be your partner, then we will find out who is."

Of course it was him. Liam was certain of it.

The other part of his curse was a hard one to break. Once the spell was written, a challenge would come in which Liam would have to put honor aside. To do so would be a betrayal to every oath he'd uttered upon becoming a knight to King James.

When John leaned forward and timidly pressed a soft kiss on his lips Liam responded immediately. When they kissed, it was as if everything ceased to exist, the problems, the curses, the entrapment. In that moment, it was just them, and the sensations only pleasure.

Liam met John's gaze. "Thank you. For everything. I do not know what else to say."

"I will wait for you and together we will work hard to free all three of you. I promise."

"I do not have anything to offer you," Liam began, but choked and couldn't continue speaking.

How was it possible to be so fortunate? Liam fought past the many emotions overcoming him. Not only the possibility to escape the entrapment, but the opportunity to openly be himself. Even if he never escaped, this moment with John would be in his memory forever. He hugged John close.

"Thank you," Liam repeated.

John sighed and wrapped his arms around Liam. "You don't have to offer me anything. I will wait. My sister will be more than happy to take over for me at the shop. She is always begging me to let her, telling me to take a holiday. She will be more than happy to have an excuse to get out of the house and be around people."

Liam stood, this time feeling the strongest tug back to the alter-world. "I must leave."

"I'll be here when you return." John told him as he disappeared.

. . .

BACK IN THE alter-world Liam filled Niall and Padriag in on what had transpired. He purposely did not divulge the possibility of his enchantment coming to an end. Neither man would give him rest, urging him to return to the other realm at every opportunity.

"So did you get a look at the people gathered?" Padriag asked. "Was there a blonde there? She will be the one with a small birthmark over her lip. Right here." He pressed a finger just above his lip.

"Most of the magics were gone when I arrived."

Padriag grunted. "You should have gone sooner."

"If someone meant for either of you was there, you would have sensed it. Did you?"

Both shook their heads.

"I tried to go but couldn't from inside the keep. I'm working on it, but Niall refuses to help me. I've tested opening a portal to the other side. Then all Naill has to do is will himself there. He won't even try." Padriag gave Niall a pointed look.

"I do not plan to leave," Niall stood and walked from the room.

Padriag watched Niall's retreat before looking to Liam. "If I leave, and you leave, what will happen to Niall?"

"I will stay here. I cannot leave him," Liam told Padriag, who frowned still looking towards the stairs.

"Shit, I guess I'll stay too."

Liam looked at the young knight. "No Paddy. You will leave when beckoned. I will speak with Niall."

He climbed the stairway, his thoughts going back to John. His lips instantly curved at recalling their short time together. The hardest part of staying in the alter-world would be never finding out what awaited him with John, but most importantly, he'd made an oath to the men he'd been with for hundreds of years. To be loyal, defend them and never leave one behind.

Niall's door was open, he peered in spotting the large man sitting on a chair, leaning forward, his face in his hands.

Not wanting to take Niall by surprise, he rapped at the door. Niall straightened, his grey eyes flat when meeting his. "What is it?"

"I am ensuring you are well." Liam hesitated, at the lack of invitation, but walked in anyway.

"I am fine," Niall replied.

Liam sat, not speaking. Over the years all of them had become accustomed to Niall's silent way.

Noticing lines around Niall's eyes, Liam wondered if the man was not sleeping. "You are tired. Can I get you something?"

"Nay, thank you."

"What do you think about when you consider the rest of us leaving you behind?"

For a long time, Niall was silent. They sat in the quiet comfort of the room for a long while, and just when Liam thought the man wouldn't reply, Niall let out a long sigh.

"I welcome the thought that you will all be freed from here and begin your lives anew."

Ensuring he kept his voice even, Liam leaned forward

and looked his friend in the eyes. "What about you? I sense your enchantress comes. She will be here soon."

"How many times have I repeated over the years. I do not wish to be free, Liam," Niall insisted. "Do not pursue it."

"Niall, you are still young, can have many years of good life with a partner, perhaps even have more children." Liam's voice hoarse with emotion. "Do not let Meliot do this to you."

Niall stood and stalked to the door. "Leave Liam. I do not wish to discuss it further."

He didn't move. "What is the real reason you prefer to remain in this horrible place? Niall, you would die here alone."

Niall went to him and grabbed him the front of his shirt, bringing his face up to his. The man's lips curved into a mirthless smile.

"With all your foresight, you should see clearly that I am already dead. I died the day I came here." With that, he shoved him out the door slamming it behind him.

Liam stood looking at the door. How would he be able to leave Niall behind?

"You are not staying here Niall," he called through the door. "I will not allow it."

Chapter Twenty-One

Long after Gwen and the others had slipped away to bed and the house fell into a hushed, breath-held silence, Sabrina sat alone in the library. A storm brewed within her—a thousand frantic thoughts, restless and relentless. How could she leave now, when so much was left undone? Self-preservation felt shamefully selfish, a betrayal. But lately, she feared she'd become more of a hindrance than a help.

And then there was Gavin.

Even now, as she tried to focus on the ancient spells spread out before her, his face, his voice, intruded on her every thought. She read and re-read the same page, words blurring, their meaning slipping through her mind like smoke. The late hour, the endless days of research—she told herself that was why she couldn't concentrate. Yet a prickling sense of urgency tugged at her, as if she'd overlooked something critical, something hidden between the lines she'd scanned a hundred times.

"Sabrina?"

Gavin's deep voice sliced through the quiet, low and dark, sending a pulse of heat through her that pooled dangerously low. Her breath hitched as his presence filled the room, unsettling the stillness with an intensity that made her grip the edge of the book. Slowly, she looked up, meeting his gaze in the shadowed doorway. His eyes held hers with an unreadable, almost primal intensity, the kind that stripped away all defenses, leaving her bare.

A shiver ran down her spine, but she fought to keep her composure, ignoring the traitorous thrum of her pulse. He was close, too close, and yet she ached for him to come closer still. She tried to speak, to make light of his presence, but her voice caught, betraying her.

In the silence, unspoken words hung heavy between them—questions she was too afraid to ask, desires she could barely admit to herself. But there was no escaping the way her body reacted to him, every inch of her attuned to his presence, every breath a little too shallow.

And as he took a step closer, his gaze unwavering, she realized that maybe she didn't want to escape.

"Come with bed. You need to leave that for tomorrow."

He held out his hand and instinctively she knew they would be going to the same bed. Her mind whirled with the implications of what going with him meant.

As if compelled by something outside her body, she stood and went to him, and took his hand, their gazes never straying. The dimness of the late hour surrounded them like a cloak, cocooning them in a world away from anything and anyone else.

Somehow, she would have to find the strength to be near him but not make love. The fact that her body hummed with anticipation didn't matter.

They entered his bedroom and Sabrina hesitated, unsure how to proceed. Would they kiss goodnight and then go to bed, each of them relegated to opposite sides.

"I have fought hard to stay away from you, but I cannot. Another night without touching you would be torture." Gavin watched her, his eyes boring into hers. "Are you afraid of me?"

"I am not afraid."

Her breath hitched as he reached for her, his fingers brushing her cheek, lingering just long enough to send a thrill through her before his mouth captured hers. The kiss was electric—a heady blend of unspoken longing and raw desire. She clutched his shoulders, letting herself fall into the kiss, as his lips moved over hers, gentle yet possessive, tasting and claiming in equal measure.

He felt perfect—every inch of him, strong and unyielding, a firm contrast to her softer curves. The press of his body against hers left her weak, trembling, as though her entire world had narrowed down to this single, intoxicating moment. She tangled her fingers in his hair, pulling him closer, needing the warmth of him, the solidness that seemed to anchor her in a way nothing else ever had.

In Gavin's arms, she felt as though she'd stepped into another world, a world where time slipped away, where nothing else mattered but this shared breath, this heartbeat thrumming in perfect sync with his own. The ancient divide between them—a lifetime, an era—vanished, swept away by the undeniable pull between them, as if they had been waiting for this reunion across centuries.

In that moment, she knew nothing else, only him—his warmth, his strength, and the consuming certainty that whatever boundaries lay between them, they were meant to be here, together, as if made for one another.

"I need ye, Sabrina," His hoarse voice vibrated against her ear.

Something inside her snapped. If she slept with him, if he were able to make love, there was no possible way she'd be able to walk away.

"I can't." Backing up and holding her hands up, she stumbled toward the doorway. "I am leaving, and this is not going to change it. I just can't do this."

Chest heaving from their kiss, hair disheveled, he looked like a god. The only obvious sign that her words affected him was the muscle in his jaw flexing. "I understand."

Sabrina ran from the room and down the stairs, desperate to find a place to be alone. Once in her bedroom, she closed the door and locked it.

Was she wrong?

Her work had always been the most important thing in her life. She'd sacrificed so much over the years, fought hard and clawed her way to become one of the most sought-after fashion photographers in the industry. If she were to choose Gavin, it would mean adjusting. It wouldn't be fair to expect him to understand her world, her having to constantly travel and work for days on end during assignments.

No, it wasn't possible. She couldn't do it. No matter how

much she loved him, there was no comparison between years of work and a relationship of only a pair of weeks.

TWO WEEKS LATER

The photo shoot wasn't going well. The client changed their mind yet again, wanting muscular models instead of slim ones. After numerous delays, they were behind schedule and Sabrina's frustration seemed to reflect in the models.

Neck tense, Sabrina waited for the male model to situate himself on top of a block of ice while Tammie tried to hide the clear mats that kept his bare back and rump, from touching the ice. The muscular male lay back allowing one arm to drape down the side of the ice, his other arm, over his head.

"Turn towards me just a bit, then arch your back and throw your head back. I want an expression of ecstasy," Sabrina called out to him. When he did as she instructed, she saw Gavin's face.

She blinked rapidly behind the camera and the model's face returned. Shaken, she took a deep breath before continuing. She couldn't keep him on the ice very long. She took a few more shots.

"That should do it," Sabrina said, stretching her neck.

Tammie chewed gum, blew out a big pink bubble and popped it before speaking. "We are not. The last model is waiting."

"Who? There were only five." Sabrina noticed Tammy bit her bottom lip.

"He got here about an hour ago. Said the client sent him. That they wanted him in the campaign."

"No one told me," Sabrina muttered, pulling her phone out to notice that indeed there was a text from the liaison insisting on a sixth model.

That's when she spotted him walking toward them wearing only a towel around his midsection. Tyler Reynolds, her ex. The man who'd broken her heart.

He spotted her and waved.

"Oh yes, wonderful to see you too," Sabrina muttered under her breath and waved back. Inwardly, she prepared herself to have a professional interaction. She'd chosen her career over Gavin and something like running into her ex, the man she was once engaged to, should be a walk in the park.

"Hello." Tyler approached, his lips curved into his familiar charming smile, his eyes sparkling. She noticed his brown hair was longer now. Although he remained as handsome as she remembered.

"How are you?" Tyler asked, his gaze scanning her face.

"Good. No time to chat. Better get to it," Sabrina stated, matter-of-factly. "Ice melts quickly." She motioned to the ice block that had been wrapped with insulation blankets after the last model.

"Right," he replied and turned to the set assistants who clasped exquisite watches on his wrists. He went to the ice block and waited for Tammie to give direction on the poses.

Once she informed him of the first pose, Tyler dropped

the towel and without a bit of hesitancy began posing. He was an expert, brought emotion and sensuality to every pose.

Sabrina realized that no matter how perfect the poses were and how sensual Tyler was, he didn't affect her like he once had. All she saw was how the shots would look to the client. Tyler definitely brought the entire campaign to life.

Once they were done, she motioned for him to get down and dress. "You did great."

Tyler gave her a quizzical look as he tugged on the robe that Tammie held out.

Can I take you for a drink?" Tyler asked, tying the velvety belt around his waist.

She considered saying no. It was probably best, but a part of her was curious to know if she was truly over him.

"I have to speak to the staff, then we can go."

"I'll get dressed." He walked back the way he'd come.

THEY ENDED up having drinks and dinner at a nearby tapas restaurant. Sabrina ordered an espresso martini, savoring the flavor as they waited for their order to begin arriving.

Tyler drank club soda. Most models didn't drink alcohol while on a shoot.

"You seem different," he told her, studying her face.

"In what way?"

He shrugged. "I don't know, relaxed maybe. Are things well with you?"

Sabrina nodded taking another sip before speaking. "My work centers me. It helps me think clearer. I am booked through next year. Everything is perfect."

"So things really haven't changed." His statement was flat, and she must have given him a disbelieving look because he continued quickly. "Don't get me wrong, what you have built is admirable. And I know how hard you work. I could never compete with it."

Tyler's words made Sabrina's breath catch. "Is that what you thought? Because I loved you, Tyler. You were very important to me."

He shook his head sadly. "I believe in your own way you did. But you never made allowances for us. I got tired of attending important events alone. You stood me up for my sister's wedding, instead accepting a last-minute job. On your birthday when I planned a trip together, you cancelled and flew to an island to do a shoot, not thinking about inviting me and that perhaps we could stay there. I lost all the money I spent on flights and the resort and when I told you, you laughed it off. Then you left me a check on the counter the next morning. Never apologized."

Sabrina couldn't believe what she was hearing. He'd never once complained, had not told her how he felt. But he shouldn't have had to.

"I am so sorry." The appeal of the food that arrived was lost as her stomach clenched at realizing how selfish she'd been.

He looked past her to the street. "I needed to get it off my chest. When you seemed blindsided by my decision to break up, I couldn't believe it. We were so disconnected that I kept expecting you to call things off."

"My heart broke," Sabrina said. "I wish you would have said something."

"I wanted to. I tried to. Every time we planned to do stuff, I was hopeful. With every cancellation I finally got to the point I gave up."

"We did stuff," Sabrina countered. "Went to parties and met friends at the bar."

"You mean your client parties?" He gave her an incredulous look. "When was the last time we met friends at the bar? I met my friends at the bar, and you popped in after a shoot if it was convenient."

"I was building my business. I thought you understood."

Tyler nodded. "I did. I really was proud of you and what you had accomplished. But I wanted to feel as if I was part of your life, not an afterthought."

She opened her mouth to tell him she'd needed someone supportive, but then realized how many times Tyler had brought her food, helped carry equipment and even stood in when her models canceled. He had done more than most men would have.

"I am truly sorry. Perhaps if you would have given me a bit more time."

"Going to my sister's wedding alone, that was the straw that broke it for me. Then you got the Ken West campaign. Knowing you were about to lose yourself in work again, I decided it was the best time for me to break things off."

Sabrina drank the rest of her martini, unable to form words. What he said was true. She'd been horrible to him. How had she been so blind. "I thought you were as passionate about my shoots as I was. You were involved in many of them."

"I became lost in all of it. Even wondering if I was in them because of my own merit or because of you."

"Damn it, Tyler. Why didn't you say something while this was happening?" Sabrina exclaimed, then lowering her voice when people at other tables looked over. "I would have pivoted, made allowances."

"Would you have?" Tyler sipped from his glass, his gaze warming. "I don't hold anything against you, but I feel it is important that you know everything I didn't get the chance to explain. We all learn from past mistakes. I learned to speak up and perhaps you won't lose another important person."

THEY BARELY TOUCHED THEIR FOOD, both giving up and hugging good-bye.

"Tyler, I wish you the best. Thank you for telling me all of this," Sabrina said, giving him another hug.

The drive to her home was short, the entire time Tyler's words repeating over and over in her head. Hearing his side of it now, she understood Tyler's decision. In his place she would have done the same.

She pulled out her keys to the front door hoping Tammie was home. Usually, after a shoot, her sister would linger with the staff to go discuss the shoot over drinks or dinner.

As soon as she entered her condo, her cell sounded. It was Gwen.

"Sabrina come back to Scotland immediately."

Her heart stopped. "What happened."

"We need your help with this. There's been very little progress. Please come and bring Tammie with you. Since you left we haven't been able to do anything about the others. Liam is refusing to allow John to help free him. Neither Padriag nor Niall have felt anything."

"How is Gavin?" She held her breath waiting for her sister's reply.

"Quiet, reserved, heartbroken. He understands that you are not obligated to be with him. But knowing it doesn't make things easier."

Sabrina was on the verge of tears. So many emotions in a matter of hours were taking their toll.

"Is he still working at the stables?"

"Oh yes. That part does distract him and keeps him busy. He's been working with Fiona's horses. She's back." Gwen groaned. "Only for a few days and already annoying me. With her around it's hard to work."

"Fiona is there?" Her voice pitched. "What the hell is she doing there?"

Gwen let out another annoyed huff. "Her competition is this weekend. She's staying in one of the cottages, keeping her distance from me. But definitely has her sights on Gavin."

A sensation of burning from the inside out made Sabrina grunt with anger. "She'd best stay away from him, or I'll yank every strand of hair from her head."

"Hey, you're the one who left," Gwen stated the obvious with a soft chuckle. "Whatever you decide about you and Gavin, I sincerely need for you and Tammie to come as soon as possible."

"I planned to return next week. We have to talk about this wedding of yours."

Tristan had insisted that he and Gwen marry, despite them trying to convince him that times were different, and it was perfectly acceptable to continue as it was. He insisted that as laird, any children that came to be could not be born out of wedlock. Gwen had given up trying to explain birth control to him.

"Have you at least made some headway in what to wear?" Sabrina asked, trying to keep from asking more questions such as how much time exactly were Gavin and Fiona spending together.

"Yes. I got a beautiful emerald green calf-length dress, it matches Tristan's eyes." Gwen sighed dramatically making Sabrina smile.

She thought of a recent conversation with their mother. "Mom is happy you're getting married, although she did express her fear that Tristan is a bit too old for you."

Both laughed.

"He is just a bit," Gwen replied with a chuckle. "She is annoyed that I will be living in Scotland, of course."

Sabrina laughed. "I am looking forward to returning. I am bringing Tammie with me, since I have an upcoming shoot in Scotland, no excuses will be accepted. I will finish up here and fly there within a couple days."

After they hung up, Sabrina began reviewing the pictures from her photo shoot. They were good, extremely good. Her picky client would be hard pressed to find fault with her idea for the males posing on ice, for their "Iceman" men's clear watch line.

She studied the one with the last model. Tyler stretched atop the ice, his head flung back as if in throes of ecstasy, one arm over his head, the other draping down the side of the block, hand fisted.

She'd posed him the entire time picturing Gavin and how he looked when she'd made love to him. He'd flung an arm over his head, his hips thrusting upward, his head back, a primal growl escaping his lips.

She took a deep breath. How she missed him.

"Hello?" Tammie called walking in. "Tell me everything. How did your drinks with Tyler go?"

Her expression must have been readable because Tammie gave her a concerned look. "Not good then?"

Sabrina smiled. "I am glad we talked. He told me things I would have never understood. I know now why he broke things off and to be honest with you, I don't blame him one bit. I wish he would have told me at the time, when things were progressively getting worse. But we can't undo the past."

"I'm glad you talked to him then," Tammie said, giving her a bright smile before eyeing the computer screen. "So how do they look? I was thoroughly enjoying having to assist the models today. Those ice poses were hot." She fanned her face with both hands dramatically.

Leaning closer, Tammie peeked at the computer screen over Sabrina's shoulder. "Wow, that one is super hot."

"And he's married. I wonder how his wife deals with such a hot husband," Sabrina remarked.

"I suppose you can find out." Tammie said giving her a knowing look. "When are you going back to Scotland?"

"In a couple days. I have to work nonstop on these and

turn them in. You will come with me because we have a shoot there."

"I thought you delayed it. Darn it. I went out again with Gerard, one of the models, for drinks and a nibble. We made a date for next weekend."

Sabrina recalled Gerard, a nice guy, one of the few models who wasn't arrogant or overly demanding. This could be problematic if Tammie was meant for one of the men in the enchantment. "Are you serious about him?"

Tammie shrugged. "Too soon to tell. It's only been a couple of dates." She changed the subject, in her usual exuberant way. "Although, I can't wait to go to Scotland. Maybe I will get to meet the knights in shining armor. I bet they're even more attractive than any of your models."

Sabrina laughed. "They are very good-looking men. Tristan is tall, dark and ruggedly handsome, and he loves Gwen, which makes him even more attractive. You'll love him."

"Tell me about your knight, Gavin."

This time she sobered, her gaze flickering back to Tyler's picture. "Gavin is beyond words. Tall, golden, and stunning. The best thing about him is that he is just as beautiful on the inside. He scares the shit out of me."

Tammie wrapped an arm around her shoulders and kissed Sabrina's temple. "You're in love aren't you?"

She could only nod as unexplained tears spilled down her cheeks.

"Damn it." She wiped them away. "I am so in love, I can't see straight."

"Aw," Tammie hugging her tight. "I know he has to be super special for you to love him."

Tammie went to the kitchen and pulled a can of carbonated water from the refrigerator. "I don't want to fall in love with one of them. I prefer a regular guy, like Gerard."

"Only you would call a male model 'a regular guy,'" Sabrina said with a chuckle. "He is one of the most exclusive and not to mention handsome models working today.

"Of the three men left, I would say Padriag is more your vibe. He's the youngest, easy-going and cute," Sabrina told her.

"Hmm," Tammie said noncommittally. "What about the other one, Niall?"

"I don't know what Niall looks like. According to Gwen he is muscular, tall, dark and super good looking, but also very somber. He is reluctant to leave the enchantment, for some reason."

Tammie wrinkled her nose. "Well, if I was his enchantress, he would be leaving the enchantment. I wouldn't give him a choice. If he wants to die that bad, he can die in Scotland, in the real world."

She tapped her foot. "I'm going to give him a piece of my mind. He has no choice, if I have to drag him kicking and screaming out of the enchantment, I will. Both my sisters' happiness hinge on that man being out of there. I know neither Gavin nor Tristan will be completely happy until they are all free."

A combination of Niall and Tammie would be interesting. Sabrina had a hard time picturing it. If Tammie was, indeed, the somber man's enchantress, Niall had no idea what was heading his way. If ever he dreamed his enchantress would be meek and mild, agreeable to letting him have his way, he'd be blindsided by the blonde with piercing aqua blue eyes that stood before her now, hands on her hips, eyebrows drawn together, plump lips pursed in thought.

Niall MacTavish wouldn't have a fighting chance.

There was no doubt about that.

Chapter Twenty-Two

The beautiful surroundings of Scotland welcomed Sabrina and Tammie as they neared Dunimarle Castle. Although Tammie had been to other parts of Europe, she'd not been to Scotland. Her expression of wonder told Sabrina that, like her, it would be easy for her sister to fall in love with the country.

"This place is magical in itself, isn't it?" Tammie asked, not waiting for a reply. "Why have I not come before? I can see how it will be a perfect place for your photography."

Sabrina scanned the landscape, green lush grass, trees and mists lingering on the craggy mountains in the distance.

"You will love the location I chose for the shots. It's actually going to be at the Campbell keep. I got all the permits."

"Oh my god. That's Gwen's new home?" Tammie's sharp intake of breath indicated they'd arrived at Dunimarle. The driver guided the car to the front of the castle and got out to open their doors.

As soon as they stepped out, Gwen came out of the house and hurried to them. "I am so glad you are both here." The sisters hugged, Gwen glancing to the doorway the entire time.

"He is not here at the moment," Gwen said, reading Sabrina's thoughts. "He is at the stables."

"With Tristan?" Gwen asked.

Gwen shook her head. "No, Tristan went with Edith to Edinburgh. Family business."

Trailing Tammie, they went inside.

"This place is amazing. I can't believe you actually live here." Tammie turned in a circle and then hugged Gwen again. "I am so very happy for you. Mom sends her best."

"How did she take you coming here?" Gwen asked.

Tammie gave a soft shrug. "I told her we were traveling for a photo shoot, and she seemed to relax a bit. She's not happy, but finally admitted she understands she can't stop me from doing what I must."

Sabrina caught Gwen's eyes. "She is still worried about Tammie coming but seems a bit less opposed."

"I'm going to explore," Tammie informed them and sprinted off, not waiting for either of them to offer to go along.

While their sister roamed, Gwen pulled Sabrina into the library. "I know you must be exhausted. But this can't wait. Tell me what your plans are. Gavin seems lost. I feel horrible for him."

Sabrina's chest constricted. "I care deeply for him Gwen, I really do. I have to decide whether or not I can be with a man whom I can't touch sexually, and then there's my work. It consumes me."

"I have a feeling that if you are truly in love with Gavin, you will make allowances. I am not diminishing the fact that it will be difficult by any means," Gwen said. "Trust yourself and have faith in what you have with Gavin. These men are strong and very intelligent. They understand this is not just an adjustment for them, but for us as well."

"Thank you. Yes, you are right," Sabrina said, looking toward the doorway. "Is Fiona still here?

Gwen nodded. "In all her annoying glory. She is usually down at the stables pestering Gavin about the horses."

"Of course she is," Sabrina replied with a droll look. "I'm going to find him."

As Sabrina steered the golf cart toward the stables, she took a deep breath, rehearsing the words she'd finally have to say. If they were going to work through things, she'd have to let her guard down and be vulnerable—a challenge she wasn't used to facing.

The stables stood in a soft hush, the earthy scent of hay and the faint musk of horse drifting through the air. Despite the windows lining each stall on both sides, the lighting remained dim, casting a tranquil, almost peaceful quality over the vast, open space.

Peering into each empty stall, she noticed that the horses had been led outside to graze and enjoy the fresh air, leaving the stables in a serene stillness that seemed to amplify her thoughts.

Voices got her attention, one sounded like Gavin, whoever he spoke to was a woman.

Sabrina followed the sound of the voices to the opposite end of the stables. Leaning against a corral fence, Fiona stood next to Gavin, both facing away.

The way Fiona glanced up at Gavin with wide eyes and a soft smile, it was obvious she meant to get his attention. "I am sure you know how to handle the feisty beast. It is just that I wanted to ensure you understood the special requirements for a show animal."

When Fiona placed a hand onto Gavin's forearm, Sabrina tensed, her eyes pinned to where the woman's hand stilled.

Gavin turned just enough that Fiona had to lower her hand. It should have made Sabrina feel better, but in that moment, she couldn't form a single thought other than wanting to rush to him and throw her arms around his neck and kiss him until they were breathless.

"The trainer informed me that he is the only one who will work with your horses," Gavin replied taking a step sideways to leave a gap between himself and Fiona. The woman was not deterred. She leaned on the fence and gazed up at him.

"You are invited to attend the competition as my guest. It will give you the opportunity to see my horses doing what they have been training to do. Plus, it would give us a chance to get to know each other better."

"I must decline your kind invitation," Gavin replied crossing his arms. "I am needed here."

"Oh, come on, Tristan told me you are part owner of these lands. You can take a day off to do something fun."

"Hey, I wasn't aware you'd returned," Sabrina lied, giving

Fiona a pointed look as she walked from the stables, pretending to have just arrived. Gavin watched her in silence.

"How are you, Gavin?" Sabrina asked with an overly bright smile.

"I am well."

Before Gavin or Sabrina could say anything else, Fiona waved toward the corral. "Of course I am here. I never am away from my horses too long. They are very attached to me and I to them. I can come and go as I please. These are my family's lands after all."

"Of course," Sabrina replied in a dismissive tone while meeting Gavin's gaze. "I was looking for you. The research we began. There have been some developments."

"We should speak then," he replied and excused himself from Fiona, who stared daggers at Sabrina.

The lack of warmth at her arrival didn't exactly surprise her, but at the same time it made for an awkward silence as they headed around the stables to where she'd left the golf cart.

"I hear you are adjusting well and enjoying your work with the horses," Sabrina said unable to take the silence any longer.

His only reply was a soft grunt and nod.

As they neared the front of the stables, he stopped and finally met her gaze. "I am glad you have returned to help. We have made little progress in freeing the others."

His coolness toward her was hurtful, but Sabrina understood. He was protecting himself.

"Right. Gwen has kept me informed. Our younger sister

came with me." Sabrina looked up at him. "I missed you. It would be nice to spend time together."

His brow creased. God was there anything that didn't make the man look more handsome? She blew out a breath to keep from throwing herself at him.

"Spend time?"

"You and I," Sabrina began. "I want to try and see if we can work past things."

When his expression remained, she wanted to scream and ask him to say something or at least give some sort of hint as to what he was thinking. Instead she bit the inside of her mouth to keep from saying something stupid.

His gaze moved from her to the scenery they passed. "I do not know what to say."

"I am so sorry for leaving so abruptly. I had a lot of thinking to do. There was work and ..." She stopped talking when his amber gaze met hers and then he nodded.

"We can speak later. Give me time to consider things. You should return to the house. I will be there shortly. Miles is expecting me to go over some ledgers." With that Gavin turned and went back inside the stables.

What if he was interested in Fiona now? Had she just lost him? Thoughts tumbled around in her head as she watched him walk back to the stables. Trudging to the golf cart, Sabrina climbed onto the seat, unable to drive away. Her vision became blurry with unshed tears. Whether they were from hurt, frustration or anger, she wasn't sure.

Perhaps all three.

The atmosphere in the library was almost cheerful. From

the way Tammie leaned forward, she was enthralled by the situation as being explained by John.

Since the last time she'd seen John, he seemed different. More self-assured and somehow more attractive. Instead of neatly combed hair, it was in a more relaxed tousled style. His button-up shirt was replaced by a black pullover that brought out the gray in his eyes. And he had an aura about him like that of a man on an important mission.

It was possible that being away from the bookstore, taking regular walks outdoors at the estate, and having a love interest had made the guy blossom.

Gwen must have noticed her studying John because she waited for him to look away and pointed to herself mouthing "I did that."

"If Liam refuses to leave, it could be what is blocking the other two. You must convince him of that," Tammie said reading notes on a paper in her hand. "I think the only way to break these curses is to do them in the specific order they present themselves by the men feeling the urge to come to this realm."

Sabrina was instantly proud of Tammie's assessment of the situation. "I have wondered if they were bewitched in a specific order and that is the way their entrapments must be broken."

"Of course! It makes sense," John agreed enthusiastically. "Our problem at the moment is that Liam hasn't appeared in a few days." He looked to Gwen for confirmation.

Their sister nodded. "Yes, today is day three."

"I can't help but fear Meliot is doing something to keep

them from escaping." John's worry made Sabrina's chest tighten.

Her fears were reflected in the others' expressions.

TRISTAN RETURNED from Edinburgh and was introduced to Tammie who gave Gwen an astounded look. "Holy...wow." Her mouth formed an O. She threw herself against him with an enthusiastic hug.

When the door to the library opened and Gavin walked in Sabrina lost her breath. Each time she saw him, he made her want to swoon like the women in the old movies. On the way to Scotland she had tried to prepare Tammie for the sight of him, but when her sister's eyes bulged and mouth went wider, Sabrina realized it was impossible.

"You are Gavin," Tammie informed him, walking up to him and staring up with wide eyes. "I can see why Sabrina is worried about life with you." She reached out and poked him in the center of his chest. "Yep, you are real."

"You are Tamara?" Gavin asked, frowning when Tammie pranced closer and touched her finger to the cleft in his chin.

"Yes. I am," Tammie said. "The youngest and most powerful of the three sisters." She held up her arms as if waiting for applause.

The men exchanged confused looks while Sabrina and Gwen grinned at their sister's antics.

"She is not the most powerful," Gwen said, grabbing Tammie around the waist. "What she is, is the most spirited."

Tristan studied Tammie. "You will be perfect for Padriag."

"That is what I was told, but I am not here to be matched with anyone," Tammie replied, extricating herself from Gwen's grasp. "First let's eat. I'm starving. I may also require a nap. Then we will kick wizard butt."

Tammie made a "follow me" motion with her right hand and marched from the room.

"I'm hungry too," John said, hurrying after Tammie.

"Good idea, let's eat." Gwen took Tristan's arm and pulled him from the room.

Chapter Twenty-Three

Holding on to each other, Liam and Padriag plopped onto the floor in the center of the keep's great room with a thud.

"That didn't work," Padriag, who remained on his back staring up at the ceiling, stated the obvious. "Why didn't it work?"

Liam flinched as he sat up. The experiment was going to cost him later. Already a huge purple bruise formed on his forearm.

"We've never tried to leap from inside because it has not worked. Perhaps we can try from the back garden, within the walls of the keep."

Niall watched from a chair. "You can no doubt leap from there, but the problem will be coming back. We cannot choose a place to land so specifically."

"If we miss the garden, we'll be dead within seconds," Padriag said.

"We have to try," Liam insisted. "The only way for us to escape is to get to the other realm."

Moments later, after surveying the area to ensure there was no one within striking distance, they walked out through the back door. Holding shields over their heads with one hand and swords in the other, Liam exited first, followed by Padriag and Niall trudged behind as they made their way to the outdoor garden.

They'd been confident of Padriag's wards when going outside, but because they needed to leap, the wards would have to be lowered for a few moments.

"Do not wait out here," Liam told Nail. "We will find a way to get inside."

Niall gave him a long dubious look before finally nodding.

"Ready?" Padriag called, out. "Three, two, one." Picturing the McRainey estate, Liam leapt.

"Umph."

Both hit the ground hard, gasping as the impact rattled through their bones. The surface was gritty, sand biting into their skin, and above them, the two glaring suns confirmed they were still trapped in the alter-world. A dark, twisting dread clawed through Liam as a vision of blood and death formed.

"Get up!" Padriag's voice was a lifeline, his grip iron as he hauled Liam to his feet.

Liam clenched his jaw. He *had* to save Padriag, to stop

the vision from coming true, even if his gift had never been wrong. This time, failure was not an option.

In the distance, the keep's turrets rose like a mirage of hope, the last beacon of safety. Their only chance.

"Run!" Liam shouted, urgency slamming into his words.

As the sound left his lips, the sand around them began to shift, twisting into unnatural shapes. Without looking back, they bolted, hearts pounding, knowing something monstrous was taking form.

No matter how fast they sprinted, the shadow continued to rise, blocking their path—a hulking, sinuous shape forming into a creature that looked like a massive eel, its gaping mouth lined with rows of serrated teeth. Dodging its snapping jaws, they pushed on, lungs burning, refusing to surrender as the creature closed in, death only a breath away.

Between running and sand, Liam's lungs felt as if they would explode in his chest. When Padriag tripped and fell, he rushed to him, doing his best to pull him up despite his legs burning from exertion.

"Do not give up," Liam screamed past the howling sounds of the sand creature that slithered toward them. "Get up."

Finally, Padriag did and they managed to jump away just as the creature's huge jaws dived over them.

"I c-can't b-breathe," Padriag gasped for air, as they circled back-to-back in order to see where the creature would come from next.

"Where did it go?" Liam wheezed out.

The sand whirled around them making it almost impossible to see. Liam tried in vain to protect his eyes, covering them and peeking between his fingers.

"Jump!" Padriag yanked him sideways, and they half stumbled for a few feet as the creature once against slammed against the ground sinking into the shifting sand.

Suddenly, they lost their footing, the sand giving way and they sunk. Both struggled, grabbing at the moving ground, trying to keep from sinking further, but it was an impossible task as they were both too exhausted to continue fighting.

Moments later Liam sank neck deep and grabbed for Padriag. "Climb on top of me. Save yourself."

Padriag's terror-filled eyes met his. "Nope." And then he sank and disappeared.

Liam screamed out his name, the sound barely audible against the creature's angry roar. Then before Liam could do anything, he too sank into the sand.

WHEN HE OPENED HIS EYES, he lay on a hard surface, the familiar purple sky above. Liam turned his head to see an unmoving Padriag lying not too far from him.

"Paddy." His voice was hoarse from thirst and the sand he must have swallowed. "Paddy, wake up."

Padriag stirred and began coughing.

Relieved, Liam lowered his head taking deep breaths of clean air. The feeling of having lived through whatever the hell had just happened was short-lived.

A circular wall appeared surrounding them and both he and Padriag struggled to get to their feet.

"What the fuck now?" Padriag rasped, looking around.

Two swords landed at their feet, and both grabbed one as they waited to see what would happen next.

No matter how exhausted, Liam would fight to the death. Meliot wouldn't win, enough was enough.

"What do you want wizard?" He called out.

Meliot floated above them, his robes swooshing around him like a billowing storm cloud.

"Did you enjoy playing in the sand?" The wizard's voice was disembodied, malevolent, the sound of it made his skin crawl.

Once again back-to-back, they waited for whatever the evil man would do next. Liam expected some sort of creatures would appear that he and Padriag would have to fight. He prayed for enough strength.

Padriag nudged him. "Why isn't he saying anything?"

The reason struck Liam. "Because I already know what he is expecting."

His friend's brow creased. "What is it?"

Liam looked to the wizard noting the challenging look. Meliot's lips curved. "Can you do it? Will you lose all honor to save yourself?"

"We will not be a spectacle for your entertainment," Liam called out. "You will never win."

The sound of Meliot's laughter and shrieks of lost souls he'd captured over centuries was so piercing, they had to cover their ears.

Meliot glided down but remained above the ground, his black eyes boring into Liam's. "In this realm, I will always be superior. I control the surroundings, and I control what appears. I can inflict pain and suffering."

In the words, Liam deciphered something important. Meliot had slipped and given him the answer he needed before proceeding.

"Will you free yourself?" Meliot called out and Padriag looked at Liam.

"What does he want us to do?" Padriag asked.

Liam shook his head. "He knows we are too tired to win a fight. Perhaps he's giving us time to rest so that we can be a bit more entertaining." He hoped Padriag believed him because he couldn't face his friend otherwise.

"For someone in a dress, you talk a lot of shit," Padriag called out to the wizard.

Meliot tilted his head, that penetrating gaze sliding from Padriag to Liam. "What will you do?"

Liam grabbed Padriag and turned him to face him. "Do you trust me?"

The younger man searched his face for a moment before nodding. "Yes, I do."

"Forgive me." In two quick moves, Liam yanked a dagger from his belt and plunged it into Padriag's heart.

"Wh-why?" Padriag's words came out like a whisper before he collapsed against Liam.

His entire body rigid with determination, Liam held his friend and lifted his gaze to the Wizard. "I know how this ends. I have the gift of foresight."

There was a questioning flicker in Meliot's expression before his lips curled into a grimace. "This was not as entertaining as I'd hoped."

Meliot faded, his eyes gazing directly at Liam. Barely able to stand from the exertion, Liam refused to release

Padriag's body. The air swirled relentlessly, as he fought against tumbling to the ground. The air was cool against his wet face. Tears streamed down his cheeks as he closed his eyes and willed himself to the keep where he would face Niall and explain why he'd had to kill their friend.

THE DARK INTERIOR of the keep's main room made for another hard landing and still Liam refused to release Padriag.

"What happened?" Niall rushed to where they lay, pulling Padriag to lay on the floor. The young knight's lips were blue, his face so pale there was no mistaking he was not alive.

After a slight hesitation, Niall leaned over Padriag and, putting his mouth over his, breathed air into him. "I will heal him," he said between puffs.

"He's dead. I killed him," Liam groaned the words out.

"I am sure you fought to save him." Niall placed both hands on Padriag's chest, doing his best to revive him. "Open your eyes Padriag. You cannot die."

Liam closed his eyes and focused using his powers of foresight for a way to change things. He'd seen it back there at the circle. Padriag alive, the young man finding his enchantress.

Had it been a trick by Meliot? No. The gift was from the enchantress who'd done her best to give them something to help them survive in the alter-world.

"Do something," Niall yelled. "Help me."

"I am trying," Liam said, moving to kneel next to Padriag to touch his cold face.

"He will not die. I saw him alive. It was the only way to break the curse. To kill him."

The fist against his face was so hard his bones cracked and Liam flew backward. "You killed him to save yourself?" Niall's expression was murderous as he swung again. Liam didn't defend himself as blow after blow came.

Each strike made his head snap backward and sideways until he could barely keep from passing out. On the stone floor, he struggled to his hands and knees.

"I had to," Liam gasped out, spitting blood.

"I will kill you before letting you be free. You have no honor," Niall swung again, and Liam waited for the blow to land.

He opened his eyes and saw why Niall hadn't struck him. Padriag stood behind him holding his wrist with both hands.

"Hey just because he killed me is no reason to beat him to pulp," Padriag said and grimaced. He frowned at Liam. "Oh, and that shit hurt. You could have stabbed me in the stomach or something."

Liam fell back, exhausted in pain, but nothing felt as strong as the relief at seeing Padriag alive. "What I suspected was right. We cannot die in this realm. He cannot kill us."

Neither man replied. Niall was hugging Padriag who grimaced. "I'm still hurt, don't squeeze me."

The sound of John's voice startled him, and Liam looked to the others wondering if they heard it.

Then everything began to fade as the tug to the other realm became stronger and stronger.

John's voice became louder and louder.

By moon's soft glow and sun's pure light,
I break the chains that bind so tight.
With breath of life and heart set free,
I call on love's sweet destiny.
The curse be gone, by ancient vow,
Let peace and passion flourish now.

"Oh my god, what happened to you?" John rushed to him when he landed in a heap inside the library in Tristan's house.

Liam sat up, his body feeling heavy and stiff. He was corporeal.

He was free.

"No. No. No." He looked around wildly as John wrapped his arms around him.

Chapter Twenty-Four

Sabrina woke from a nap with a start. She'd wanted to talk to Gavin, but exhaustion from the flight to Scotland and staying up late to get pictures edited had finally taken its toll.

When she'd finally gotten Gavin alone in the library, she'd barely begun her practiced speech when Gavin told her he needed time to consider things. She'd not stopped him. After all, she was the one who'd left and not allowed them time to work things out. It was only fair to move forward on his terms.

There seemed to be a lot of activity on the first floor. There was loud talking and even clapping below. Whatever happened, was causing excitement.

Perhaps Liam had finally been able to reappear. Sabrina sprang from the bed and rushed to the bathroom to rinse her face and run a comb through her hair. She'd gone to bed wearing a gray long sleeve t-shirt and matching athletic leggings. Since she wore socks, her footsteps were silent as she hurried down the stairs.

Everyone was in the library. On the couch was a bloodied Liam, John beside him. Tammie held a bowl of wet washcloths and Gwen was wiping Liam's face.

Gavin and Tristan looked on with concerned expressions.

"What happened to him?" Sabrina asked, moving to stand next to Gavin.

"His curse has been broken," Gavin informed her.

She leaned into him and whispered. "Why doesn't anyone look happy? Who beat him up?"

It was Gwen who spoke next. "Liam is not happy to have left the other two. Niall beat him up."

They filled her in on what had happened. When they got to the part of Liam having stabbed Padriag, Sabrina gasped. "Oh no. That had to be awful for you."

Liam closed his eyes.

"What do we do next?" Tammie asked. "Maybe he should take a shower. There's sand everywhere."

"Can you stand?" John asked the injured man who nodded.

John and Tristan helped Liam to stand, and when he seemed steady enough they helped him from the room.

"Should we call a doctor?" Tammie asked. "He said one of his ribs might be cracked."

Gwen shook her head. "Miles went to get his bag. He is a trained paramedic. Said he will stitch up the cuts and tape his ribs." Just then the aforementioned man walked in with a white case. "Where'd he go?"

"Up to take a shower," Tammie said pointing to the ceiling.

The older man hurried from the room and up the stairs.

"Tammie, let's make some dinner. The staff is off today. It's been a crazy day." Gwen tugged her sister from the room giving Sabrina a pointed look.

Noting Gavin's worried expression, his gaze toward the stairway, Sabrina went to him and instinctively wrapped her arms around his waist. "He will recover from his injuries. I am sure of it."

His arms came around her, but his body remained still.

"I'm sorry, I wasn't thinking," Sabrina tried to push away, but his arms remained solidly around her.

"I do not mind." Gavin peered down at her. "We should talk."

Sabrina's heart thundered wildly. This was it. She would put everything on the line, make sacrifices that she'd never thought to have to make. Letting out a shaky breath, she allowed Gavin to pull her over to a pair of chairs next to a wide set of windows. From there, the view of the rolling hills, trees and lazily grazing sheep gave the illusion that everything was, and would be, well.

Fingers intertwined to keep her hands from shaking, Sabrina swallowed. "I am going to move here, to Scotland. To be with you."

He started to speak, but she held up a hand. "Let me finish, please, before I lose my nerve." Sabrina blew out a breath. "I am in love with you Gavin. I have no idea how that is possible after such a short time, but I have absolutely no doubts. I love you like I've never loved anyone before."

There was a combination of uncertainty and hope in his eyes. "I owe you my life Sabrina. I do not expect anything from you. It is I who should make sacrifices for you. I can go to where you live and do whatever it is I can to make life easier for you."

Her heart melted for him. Transitioning to life in the Scotland countryside would be hard enough. She couldn't imagine him in the busy city of Atlanta.

"I want to live here. In my job, I can work from anywhere in the world. Is it agreeable to you that I come to live here?"

Gavin nodded. "Aye, I would like that verra much."

Her heart leapt in her chest. He'd not said how he felt, which was fine. They'd come to that topic later. First, she needed to finish telling him everything.

"I want to tell you more," Sabrina continued. "My work takes me away for many days at times, to distant locations. For the foreseeable future, I have cancelled some shoots. But when I do go to work, I hope you will travel with me."

"Will we travel on those air...cars?" He pointed to the sky.

"Airplanes. Yes, we may have to."

"I wish to do that," Gavin replied with a grin.

Sabrina wanted to leap up and throw herself against him, but she held back. "I do want there to be intimacy between us. I cannot be in a relationship without it. I don't mind us taking it slowly, but we will have to work on me being able to touch you during sex."

Gavin nodded. "I will do anything to keep you in my life. I cannot see going forth without you in it."

Batting her eyelashes at him, Sabrina leaned forward. "Gavin, you like me, you really, really like me?"

"Do not a jest. I do care deeply for you, perhaps I love ye." Gavin attempted to look serious, but his lips curved. "Ye...er, you are a minx."

"I want to be your minx," Sabrina leaned forward, he did the same and they kissed.

BY THE EVENING, Liam was well enough to join them for dinner. The Englishman brooded the entire time, feeling too guilty to appreciate his freedom. The conversation during the meal centered on how to free Padriag and Niall. It would take time and patience which, after freeing three of the men, everyone was not feeling.

Sabrina got everyone's attention. "From what I understand, neither Padriag nor Niall have felt the urge to leap here. Is it possible, we may have to search further for their helpers?"

She glanced at Gavin and then to Tristan. Both had the same look of quiet desperation. They wouldn't be able to rest fully until their friends were also freed.

"We will continue to work hard to bring them to this world," Gwen said to the others at the table. "There are four of us here who will not give up."

"Work begins at dawn," Tammie said with a firm nod. "I have some ideas."

John reached for Liam's hand, squeezing it. "We will free them, have no doubt."

When Liam looked at John, Sabrina could see the growing bond between the men. She looked to Gavin who watched the pair with a soft smile.

AFTER A SHOWER, Sabrina sank into her bed. Usually she'd be surrounded by photo proofs and electronics, on which she'd work until falling asleep. This night, despite not feeling sleepy, she sank back against the pillows and closed her eyes considering the events of the day.

Gavin, Tristan and Liam had been deep in conversation when she'd gone to the library and kissed Gavin good night. The men were discussing different scenarios, reverting to old English as they considered the fate of the two men left behind. It was no use to tell them to get rest.

What would happen if the last two men could not be freed?

It was a depressing thought, but a possibility none of them wanted to accept. The Magic Book was on her night table. Interesting as she'd last seen John with it. Perhaps someone had brought it to her room.

Picking up the heavy tome, she leafed through it, stopping every so often to scan the words on the page. Spells could be read, but not out loud, which made finding the right one difficult at times.

The door opened and Gavin walked in, his gaze moving from her to the book. "Can I join you?"

Closing the book and putting it back on the end table, she patted the bed. "Of course you can. I would love it."

He went to the bathroom emerging a few minutes later wearing only boxer briefs. She suspected Miles had spent time with both Tristan and Gavin explaining hygiene for the current times, because Gavin's hair was damp from the shower.

Unable to look away, she took him in. One day she'd do a photo shoot of him. If he allowed it.

The bed dipped under his weight, and he lay back on the pillows, both hands under his head, eyes to the ceiling.

"There's so much happening. I can only imagine your mind is racing," Sabrina murmured.

Gavin turned to her, then glanced back up at the ceiling. "I'm grateful for Liam's freedom. But we cannot stop until Padriag and Niall are free as well."

Sabrina reached over, her fingers grazing his hand. "None of us will rest until it's done. You have my word."

After a pause, Gavin let out a long sigh. "Niall...he doesn't want to be saved."

"Then we won't give him a choice," Sabrina said softly, turning to face him. "He, like you and the others, deserves his freedom."

His gaze lingered on her lips, and she leaned closer, her heart beating faster as she brushed her mouth against his in a gentle kiss. "Try not to worry too much. I know it's hard, but we need to keep our minds clear for what lies ahead."

They were silent for a few moments, each searching the other's eyes, their breaths mingling. Then, with a quiet intensity, Gavin leaned in, capturing her lips in a deeper kiss that sent her heart soaring.

After a moment, he drew back, his expression tender and uncertain. "Can we ..." He hesitated, choosing his words carefully. "I want to be with you."

Sabrina's pulse quickened, and she couldn't hide her smile. She had tried so hard to keep her hopes at bay, but now, with his confession, her own longing broke free.

"I want to be with you, too," she whispered, their hands entwining as they finally allowed the walls between them to fall.

He needed no further encouragement, immediately shifting over her, his mouth taking hers with fervor. There was no better way to push through hard emotions than with sex, in Sabrina's opinion.

She wiggled out of her tank top, and he pushed down her pajama shorts, leaving her fully bare beneath him. With deep kisses, his mouth teased hers, moving from the corner of her lips down to her throat. Sabrina clutched the sheets, pushing her head back against the pillow.

Don't touch him. She repeated the words mentally when his mouth clamped around her left nipple, his hands sliding up her sides, cupping both breasts.

The more he continued the wonderful explorations with both his mouth and hands, the harder it was to keep from raking her nails down his back.

"I need you now," she gritted out, her core an inferno of heat.

"Oh!" She moaned out the word when finally he reached between them and guided himself to her sex.

Sabrina let out a deep, guttural moan when he sank fully into her. When he began moving, his hands on her hips, Sabrina couldn't keep herself in check. Immediately, her body reacted to the feel of him.

The centuries between them had definitely not made a difference when it came to lovemaking, because Gavin was good, very good. Seeming to sense her body's needs, he caressed, kissed and nipped wherever it was needed. Not only was he good, but the lovemaking lasted longer than she expected. Both taking turns driving the tempo.

Nearing the brink Sabrina grasped the bed linens so hard, her fingernails dug into her palms. Then she lost all control, coming with so much force, she lost her ability to breathe.

Heat traveled through her body, searing a path of wonderful sensations. Unable to fight it, she let go, floating as waves of passion flowed.

"Sabrina," Gavin's hoarse voice permeated through the fog, and he shuddered and collapsed.

"Mmm," she murmured against his ear. "You are a great lover." Sabrina wanted to nibble the earlobe, but wondered if that would be pushing it, so she resisted.

Gavin lifted and stared down at her. "You touched me."

"Wh-what?" Sabrina attempted to move from under him, but didn't make any progress. "I don't think I did." She lifted her hands as if it proved anything. "I was grabbing the blankets the entire time, I promise."

Lifting an eyebrow, he gave her a wicked smile. "I am sure you did not keep your hands or mouth to yerself." He rolled off of her and motioned to the left side of his neck.

There was no mistaking what the red mark was. It was huge.

"Oh my god. I gave you a hickey."

Frowning he turned to her. "What is a hickey?"

"A love bite."

He shrugged. "I do not mind." Then he rolled to his side to look at her. "I enjoyed it. It didn't bother me. Quite the opposite."

"Seriously." Sabrina was sure her eyes looked about to pop from her head. "You didn't feel fear or anger? You didn't have some kind of moment that you feared you might lose control?"

He shook his head. "No. I enjoyed it, wanted you to continue." Once again the corners of his lips lifted. "I did lose control."

"That is certainly good news." Sabrina lifted up and inspected the mark on his neck. "I can't believe I did that. I am thirty years old for goodness sakes." She covered her face with both hands. "My sisters are going to roast me alive."

At his frown, she explained what she meant.

"Come." Gavin spread out his arms and she snuggled against his side, her head on his shoulder.

"Do you think it's safe for us to fall asleep with me like this?"

Gavin pressed a kiss to her lips. "I will move away before I fall asleep."

Against his body, in his arms, Sabrina knew all would be well. They'd conquered the hardest part, freeing him. The other things would fall into place. It was the first time in her life that she didn't worry about deadlines, about work or what happened in the fashion industry.

In Gavin's arms, all she felt was security, safety and contentment. If only she never had to move from his embrace, it would be a delightful place to live.

When she heard his breathing soften, she shifted and looked at him. He was fast asleep. She chuckled and gently moved from his arms. As much as she wanted to wake snuggled against him, she'd rather be safe than dead.

Sabrina slid from the bed, pulled a blanket from the top of the closet and rolled it to make a makeshift barrier down the center of the bed. Gavin didn't move the entire time she worked. He was exhausted and needed the rest, apparently.

Sabrina climbed back into the bed and settled on her half.

As she was falling asleep, Gavin's arm came to rest around her waist.

CHAPTER TWENTY-FIVE

Liam woke with a start. He sat up and looked around the unfamiliar surroundings. He was in a strange bed, in a room he'd never been in. When he started to sit up, his body reminded him of the day before. The entire region from his face to his abdomen protested any movements.

When Niall became free, perhaps he could fight for a living. The man was powerful when furious.

Moving slowly, Liam sat up and swung his legs to the side of the bed. He wore a sleeveless shirt and pants made of thin fabric. He assumed it was what people wore to sleep during the present time. Admittedly the clothing was comfortable.

After relieving himself, he searched for something to wear. The only thing that he found was a robe of sorts that had been left folded over a chair.

Knocks sounded and Liam shrugged on the robe.

"Liam, are you awake?" John called softly. The sound of the man's voice made his stomach jump.

"I am," he replied, watching as the door opened and John entered with a tray. He stopped short at seeing him standing.

"You should wait for the doctor who will be coming later this morning before being up and about."

John was careful around him. He wouldn't describe it as timid, but more as if he measured every movement. Although he'd not been with anyone sexually in centuries, Liam was a passionate man. Already there was a palpable attraction between them. Hopefully soon, the physical aspect of their relationship would blossom past kissing.

"Help me to the bed," Liam said, a subtle edge to his voice as he watched John closely.

"Yes, of course." John set the tray down and moved toward him. "Let me take your arm. You're bruised—I don't want to cause you more pain."

But before John could reach him, Liam gripped his shoulders, his intense gaze locking onto John's. "Tell me," he murmured, voice low, "are you uncertain about me?"

"Uncertain?" John hesitated, his eyes searching Liam's face. "Well...yes. A bit. I'm not quite sure what to make of you," he admitted, his tone caught between caution and curiosity. "You're...a hard man to read."

Tension thickened the air between them, each unspoken question pulling them closer to a truth

John appealed to every part of him. He was slender but built perfectly, with a trim waist and well-formed backside.

"I am very attracted to you," Liam said allowing his gaze to linger on John's lips. "You are not indifferent to me."

John's lips curved. "No, I am not indifferent to you. I am also practical and know that at the moment you have broken bones and, well, other than kiss you, anything else could cause you pain."

Not waiting for Liam to say anything else, John cupped his face and kissed him. The kiss was not at all what he'd expected. Not gentle or uncertain, but hard, passionate and promising.

Liam parted his lips to allow the intrusion of John's tongue. He inhaled sharply and it hurt, but the pain seemed to evaporate when John broke the kiss and trailed his tongue to the side of his neck and nipped his ear. "I want you so much," John whispered.

It was all he could do not to lose it then and there. Instead, Liam clung to John's shoulders, his body taut with want.

John broke the kiss and Liam stared at the handsome man's lips. Those lips had been on his.

"What do you want right now?" John asked, his eyes darkening. "My lips on you?"

Brain addled, he could only nod, doing his best to let out shallow breaths at the friction of fabric against his skin when John pushed his pants down past his knees.

"Sit on the bed," John said taking his hand.

Liam allowed himself to be guided, the fog in his head threatening to take over at the idea that for the first time in so long, he was being kissed, touched. He was so hard it was almost painful.

When John dropped to his knees, Liam almost whimpered with anticipation.

"I have been dreaming of this." John met his eyes as he took him into his mouth. The heat and wetness of John's mouth as he took him deep made Liam groan low in his throat. It was a sensation like nothing he remembered. He peered down not wanting to miss a second of the erotic moment.

Liam kept his breathing shallow and constant, enjoying the view as he slid in and out from between John's lips.

"I AM surprised you lingered so long before coming downstairs," Tristan said when Liam entered the front room later that morning after seeing the doctor.

Gavin looked up and met his gaze. Liam's steps faltered. It was so different seeing Gavin now. Easier.

The men watched him closely. He knew they worried about his injuries. However, they also knew him better than he knew himself and would not offer help as it would annoy him.

"We are considering trying to summon Padriag and Niall ourselves, although we are not Magics we do come from that realm," Gavin said.

When Liam didn't reply, Gavin met his gaze and then spoke to Tristan. "We will continue this later?"

Tristan nodded, seeming to understand Liam needed a moment.

"Come outside with me." Gavin said, walking from the room at a normal stride that meant Liam had to walk faster than his bruised body allowed.

. . .

ONCE OUTSIDE, Liam took a lungful of air. His ribs protested, but he didn't care. Both he and Gavin looked up at the sky. It was so different from the purplish hues of the alter-world. Although a bit cloudy, the blue sky was so beautiful it made Liam blink back tears.

"I never thought to be here again. So familiar and yet so very different," Gavin said. "Every morning I wake expecting to be back there and that this was just a dream."

They walked down a slight hill, their pace purposely slow and without a destination in mind. When they came to a fence surrounding where the horses were kept, Liam placed his hands on it and bowed his head.

"Are you in pain?" Gavin asked.

"No." Liam squeezed his eyes shut in a futile effort to keep tears at bay. He didn't want to break down. A knight always kept his emotions in check. He was about to lose control, and it wasn't to his liking.

"I need to be alone." The attempt to keep his voice steady failed.

"Not right now. You are hurting. I do not know what happened when you left. Liam, we are forced to face incredible obstacles to become free."

Liam whirled to Gavin, no longer caring that the tears flowed down his face. "I lost my honor. I betrayed a friend to gain my freedom. I am no better than Meliot.

"What happened had to happen. You said Paddy is alive and well."

"It could have been a trick. Meliot could have made me see an outcome that was not to be true. Padriag could have been dead."

Gavin's expression turned hard, his lips twisting with anger. "The wizard is not aware of what the enchantress gifted us with. You trusted in your power. You saved yourself and Padriag from further suffering. I am sure Padriag has forgiven you. He trusted you. Now you must forgive yourself."

Upon becoming a knight in the king's court, Liam had given his word, swore to be honorable above all things. To protect and to remain above reproach. He was a failure in every way. From his attraction to men, to the constant battles with Gavin and then finally the betrayal of a man who was like a brother to him.

"I am no longer an honorable man."

Gavin looked at him for a long time. "I disagree. You would give your life for every one of us. You love freely despite what others would condemn you for. Even when we fought constantly, I never doubted that you would protect me from harm during the many useless quests we faced."

The golden knight placed a hand on Liam's shoulder. "I have and will always admire you."

Liam collapsed against Gavin and sobbed. Every ounce of pain and shame washing through his battered body and spirit. Strength emanated from Gavin when his arms surrounded Liam. A soothing warmth surrounded him, and he reveled in it. The sensation was like that when Niall healed them. Moments later Liam took a deep breath.

Tristan came up placing hands on both their shoulders. "This was not something I would have ever pictured. You two being kind to one another. I am glad to see it."

Liam turned away and wiped his face. "Do not expect to see it again. He is still the most irritating person I know."

"Have you given thought to where you wish to live?" Tristan asked Liam, joining them at the fence.

"When going to Edinburgh with Edith, I began the process of installing the gold I saved for each of you into what is called a bank. It is a place that holds coffers."

He shook his head. "The way purchases and sales are done now is very strange, but I am slowly coming to understand it."

Unsure what it all meant, Liam gave Tristan a confused look. "What do you mean gold for each of us?"

Tristan gave Liam a curious look. "The bruises from your face are gone."

Startled, Liam reached up to his face realizing the pain from his midsection was gone as well and he was breathing without pain. He gave Gavin a grateful look. "It seems my wounds are healed."

Gavin looked to each of them. "Was it me?"

"Seems it was," Tristan said with a grin.

Liam closed his eyes and willed himself a short distance away.

THE THREE MEN strolled along a path lined with trees and grazing horses as Tristan explained the intricacies of banking. Not only would each of them be well established financially, but, as it turned out, they would be incredibly wealthy—the gold bars he'd hidden were worth a fortune.

On their way back, Liam looked toward the house. "I

wish to travel to England once all is sorted. Return to live there. I will have to discuss it with John, but I expect he will not have any objections."

Tristan laughed. Then at Liam's confused expression, he explained. "Do not assume that you will be as convincing with your partners as you were when you first lived here. There are no hierarchies in this society. He does not have to do as you say based on your knighthood."

Liam grunted.

These were most confusing times indeed.

Chapter Twenty-Six

"Good news," Gwen said walking into the library. "Fiona is gone. She found our company extremely boring, according to Edith."

Sabrina sat back and rubbed her eyes. Both John and Tammie looked as tired as she felt. Papers with notes and spells that had proved to be useless were scrunched and scattered on the floor. The one trash bin they'd put beside the table overflowed with torn and crumpled paper.

The whiteboard that had been set up had lists with almost every item on them, crossed off. The sounds were those of pens scratching across paper, the ticking of the antique clock on the far wall and every once in a while someone mumbled words.

"This is ridiculously difficult," Sabrina said out loud leaning back in on the overstuffed chair where she'd been reading notes.

"We have to come up with something soon, time is

passing and the men left behind are vulnerable." Tammie stretched, arching her back.

John followed suit rounding his shoulders. "I think we may be trying too hard. Perhaps instead of this," he said pointing to all the notes and books. "We should concentrate on our senses, use our abilities without expectation of a spell, but instead a supernatural directive."

"You may be on to something there," Tammie said. "After lunch, let's separate, each of us alone and try that."

Tristan, Gavin and Liam walked in. The expressions of excitement made Sabrina and those at the table sit up straighter.

"What is it?" Sabrina asked.

"We have retained some of our gifts," Tristan said. "Different ones actually. Gavin can heal, and Liam can move himself to other places."

It was then she noted that Liam's face was free of bruising, and he stood straight, not seeming to be in pain.

"Can you go back to the alter-world?" Gwen asked, her eyes wide.

Liam shrugged. "I am about to try. I willed myself to the front of the house and it was easy. We wanted you to be aware of what had occurred before I tried. He met John's eyes.

John got up and went to Liam. "Are you sure about this? What if you cannot return?"

"I will return. My spell is broken." He gave John a warm look. "I must try."

"Can we do something to help?" Tammie asked. "I don't know, some sort of ward or spell to keep you protected?"

By the looks exchanged, everyone was energized again. Things were progressing, now they had to formulate a plan. A way to keep not only Liam safe, but to find how to break both Niall and Padriag from their entrapment.

"We have to think it through," John said.

Sabrina took Gavin's arm. "First we will eat and discuss things. We have to come up with a plan."

"Please give us the rest of the day to figure out a ward," Tammie insisted.

LIAM RINSED his face and studied the image in the mirror. He was still the same as he'd been all those years. He'd been three and thirty when entering the enchantment. Icy blue eyes met his, and he studied the man he had become. Unshaven and with slight lines between his brows and on the outer corners of his eyes, he looked older. Good. He was glad to see that the trials of the many years trapped had left their mark.

The soft jawline of his youth was replaced by a strong square shape. He'd never been a vain man as he considered vanity to be a flaw. He ran a comb through his hair sweeping it away from his face.

He'd have to get it cut to look more the way it was worn currently.

John came up and studied him in the mirror. "Do you prefer your hair long?"

A good segway into the conversation Liam wished to have. "How is hair worn currently?"

Tilting his head, the handsome man studied him. "I think longer hair is nice, but a shorter cut suits your demeanor better. By the way you carry yourself, I would guess you will prefer to wear tailored clothing."

"I had a tailor before," Liam agreed. "I always wore my hair shorter. I will leave it up to you to help me with that."

John smiled. "It will be my pleasure. But that is not what I want to talk about. I want to discuss your plan to try to go back. This is not a decision that you can make alone. Did you not consider how I would feel about it?"

Unsure how to react, Liam remained silent for a beat. He'd never been in a relationship before and had never observed one between two men. In truth, he wasn't sure what the rules were for the current times.

"I do hope you agree with me. That I must do everything possible to help free my brethren."

Seeming to understand, John took his hand and led him to sit on the bed. "I do understand. What I wish to clarify is that I want to be with you, to have a relationship with you. If you feel the same and wish to remain with me, we will have to discuss important decisions together."

Feeling his eyes widen, Liam's stomach clenched. "Of course I want to be with you. You and I are meant to be."

"That is not the answer I was hoping for," John said, hurt in his eyes. "Liam, I do not want you to feel duty bound to me."

This was becoming a complicated conversation. Liam searched for the right words to express himself. "I have never...I have never been in a relationship before. Yes, I have had intimate relationships with men and women before the enchantment. But never something long-lasting."

John's face softened, his gaze searching Liam's. "Go on."

"Through all this uncertainty, I have no doubts about one thing and that is that I want to be with you. Whether it is here in Scotland, England or any place else. You are the most important thing to me other than freeing my brothers."

The man he was undoubtedly in love with considered Liam's words and then lifted his gaze to meet his. "I understand you will stop at nothing to free them. I admire it. It scares me, the thought of losing you so soon after meeting, but I cannot stand in your way."

Not only was he fortunate enough to be free from so many years of being held captive, but now he was gifted the opportunity of love. A love he would have never dreamed off. For the second time that day, Liam fought against the same fear.

"I will vow to return to you then." Liam took John's mouth with intensity, their lips colliding with the passion of newly declared love.

"You are fully healed?" John asked breathlessly, a sly grin forming. "No pain at all?"

Liam pushed him back onto the bed. "I am fully able."

AFTER THE MEAL, they'd decided to separate, find a spot that felt comfortable and consider what to do next.

A task much easier said than done, Sabrina thought as she paced the front room, unsure if this was the space where she would sense what to do next. More than anything she felt restless and decided to try the back garden.

It was a pleasant day, the sun bright in the cloudless sky. Although there was a brisk wind, it didn't diminish the warmth.

She stopped short when she spotted Tammie sitting on the ground, eyes closed, her face up to the sky.

Sabrina's lips curved at how perfect the setting was. Looking like a water sprite in flowing blue skirts and a lacy top, her petite sister fit there. It felt as if Tammie was meant to be in that exact place at that precise time, the wind ruffling the golden strands, whilst she sat perfectly still, waiting to hear, to sense.

Turning, Sabrina tiptoed back the way she'd come, not wanting to disturb Tammie.

Gavin had gone to the stables, claiming he thought better when with the horses. She understood, because it was the one place that remained the same. No distractions by modern things like cell phones or computers.

In the distance, she saw him standing by a corral, his attention turned toward the view of hills and valleys in the distance. She felt compelled to go to him, sensing he needed her.

"Hey, you," she greeted when nearing. "You seem deep in thought."

Gavin turned to her, his lips lifting into a smile. "I keep seeing the surroundings and losing my breath at the beauty that Scotland remains."

"You haven't been to the cities yet. It will be surprising to you."

"Aye, Tristan has told me. He says it is like an entirely different world."

She came to stand next to him and he pulled her against his side. "We will start with the local village and ease you into the rest slowly."

"I am not a wee bairn to be coddled," Gavin said. "The sooner I begin to learn, the more useful I can be with having to help everyone."

Sabrina chuckled. "You are brave. I can picture what a great leader you were as laird."

Turning her to face him, Gavin kissed her, his lips lingering across hers. Sabrina lifted her arms, wrapping them around his neck and pressed her body against him. He was her golden knight, the one who brought out the best version of her.

She would fight with all her might for his happiness, which meant stopping at nothing to save the two men still trapped.

"I have never felt like this," Gavin said peering into her eyes. "I am in love with you Sabrina."

Pressing another soft kiss to his lips, Sabrina grinned up at him. "You make my heart happy."

The ground seemed to shift, and Sabrina was sure she would've fallen sideways if not clinging to Gavin.

Gavin and everything around them disappeared to be replaced by a dark stone walled chamber. Sabrina turned in a circle taking in the surroundings. It was definitely not her realm.

Movement caught her attention, and she whirled to see a

dark-haired man standing with his back to a corner, arms outstretched as if protecting himself.

Before him stood a beautiful woman, the expression on her face one of sorrow. When the woman took a step toward the man, he collapsed to the floor and scrambled backward.

It seemed as if neither of them saw or noticed her, so she stayed silent.

An outline formed behind the man and just as he turned toward it, shadows fell over the pair. Seeming alarmed, both turned toward it and vanished.

"What is it?" Gavin's voice broke the trance. "Are you unwell?"

Sabrina blinked adjusting to the light. "I had a vision. Oh my god." She grabbed Gavin's arm.

"I think I know who will save Niall. And I think I also know why he has not been forthcoming in how to break his spell."

"Let us go tell the others," Gavin took her hand.

When she didn't move, and he turned to her about to question the reluctance.

"I am scared."

Wrapping his strong arms around her, Gavin pressed his cheek against her brow. Instantly, the anxiety lifted.

"We are stronger together and will grow stronger with the others," Sabrina murmured. "But we have to prepare ourselves for a fight."

"That is why Liam must return to the alter-world. So that Meliot is not aware of the fact his curse has been broken. He will be a weapon and a way to help the others," Gavin said with assurance.

Sabrina nodded. "We will free them. I have no doubts."

They looked to the house and then to each other. "Do you think the others are getting visions as well?" Gavin asked.

"I do." Sabrina took his hand. "Tomorrow we will begin anew."

Gavin straightened, standing tall, his façade that of a warrior. "Yes."

"I love you," Sabrina said leaning against him. "I am so happy to share all this with you. Soon this will be over, and we will live here in this beautiful place together."

"I love you as well," Gavin replied his amber gaze seeming to glow with the warmth emanating from it.

Across from where they stood, the castle stood proud. Both watched as Tammie walked from the garden toward the front of the castle. She hesitated for a moment and then turned in a circle, arms up to the sky.

She looked to Gavin, and he nodded in understanding.

Tammie was about to become a hero.

"We will keep her safe," Gavin assured.

Knowing there were no assurances, Sabrina let out a long breath and leaned against the man she would love and draw strength from for the rest of her life.

ALSO BY HILDIE MCQUEEN

An Enchanted Knight

A Beautiful Knight

CLAN ROSS

A Heartless Laird

A Hardened Warrior

A Hellish Highlander

A Flawed Scotsman

A Fearless Rebel

A Fierce Archer

CLAN ROSS OF SKYE

The Wolf

The Hawk

The Raven

The Falcon

GUARDS OF CLAN ROSS

Erik

Torac

Struan

CLAN ROSS OF THE HEBRIDES

The Lion

The Beast

The Eagle

The Fox

The Stag

The Duke

The Wildcat

The Hunter

The Bear

ROGUES OF THE LOWLANDS

A Rogue to Reform

A Rogue to Forget

A Rogue to Cherish

A Rogue to Ensnare

HISTORICAL SCOTTISH NOVELLAS

Declan's Bride: A Highland Romp

Ian's Bride: A Highland Rom 2

The Lyon's Laird

Medieval Highlander Romance: The Seer

PIRATES OF BRITANNIA

The Sea Lion

The Sea Lord

A Different Shade of Blue

The Darkest Blue

Every Blue Moon

Blue Horizon

Montana Blue

Midnight Blue

Shades of Blue Boxed Set

Blue Montana Christmas

HISTORICAL WESTERN ROMANCE

Judith, Bride of Wyoming

Patrick's Proposal

WESTBOUND SERIES

Where the Four Winds Collide

Westbound Awakening

THE FORDS OF NASHVILLE

Even Heroes Cry

The Last Hero

Nobody's Hero

THE MORIAG SERIES

The Beauty and the Highlander

The Lass and the Laird

Lady and the Scot

The Laird's Daughter

HIGHLAND MEDIEVAL ROMANCE

Highlander - The Archer

The Duke's Fiery Bride

CONTEMPORARY & WESTERN ROMANCE

Melody of Secrets

Taming Lisa

Cowboy in Paradise

About the Author

USA Today bestselling author Hildie McQueen brings action, romance, and unique settings to life in her captivating stories. From sweeping Scottish historical romance to thrilling contemporary romances, her books offer something for every reader to devour!

When she's not weaving tales, Hildie loves diving into a good book, connecting with fans at events, exploring new places, and spending time with her three adorable pups. She lives in the charming small town in Georgia with her superhero husband, Kurt, who makes every day an adventure.